For Tracey Wade,
In a world full of plow horses,
Behold! a unicorn.

With grateful acknowledgment

To Martha Bessey, who sent me a wonderful collection of material on the town of Chester, Vermont, which served as a template for my town of Willams Crossing. Trust me, the real Chester has a much better police force.

Thanks very much,
Mark Sumner

THE GLOBAL QUERY

"WE BRING YOU NEWS FROM THE EDGE!"

Featuring one of the best
investigative reporters in the business:
SAVANNAH "SAVVY" MCKINNON!

THE MONSTER FROM MINNESOTA

When Savvy gets a phone tip about four mysterious deaths in northern Minnesota, her instincts tell her to follow up. Sure, maybe the people were killed by the lake monster known as Big Jelly. But Savvy thinks something—or someone—else did the dirty work . . .

". . . offers plenty of potential for a series." —*Locus*

". . . perfect for an afternoon's entertainment." —*SF Site*

". . . blends science fiction with mystery in a satisfying investigative story . . ." —*The Bookwatch*

"Sheer entertainment . . ." —*The Midwest Book Review*

INSANITY, ILLINOIS

The *Global Query* is being bombarded with obscene phone calls! Well, maybe not obscene, but calls from a housewife attacked by appliances and a man with snow geese in his toilet are definitely peculiar. Savvy realizes that these bizarre tales are all originating from the same small Illinois town. Is it mass hysteria or mass hypnosis? Savvy starts to dig for the truth—which places her in grave danger . . .

"Fast-paced, amusing." —*Locus*

"I hope Savvy stays around for many more adventures!" —*Science Fiction Chronicle*

NEWS FROM THE EDGE

THE TRUTH EXACTLY THE WAY YOU WANT IT

Ace Books by Mark Sumner

NEWS FROM THE EDGE: THE MONSTER OF MINNESOTA
NEWS FROM THE EDGE: INSANITY, ILLINOIS
NEWS FROM THE EDGE: VAMPIRES OF VERMONT

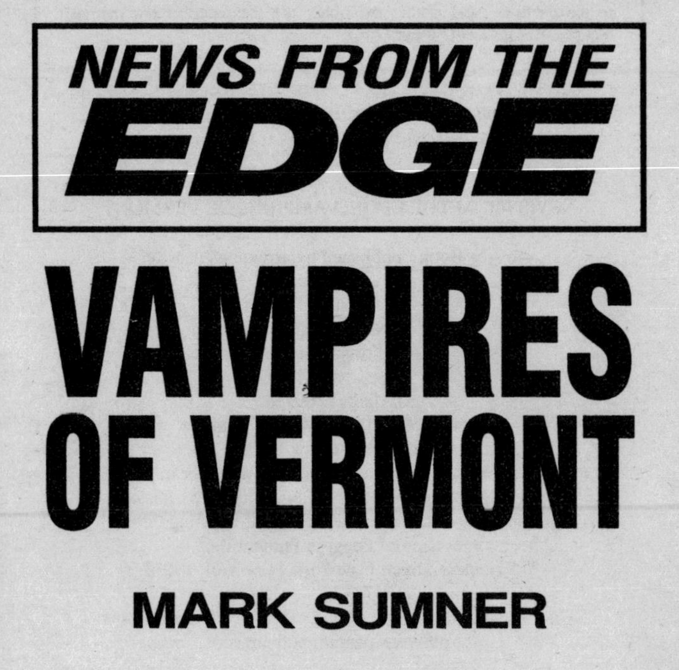

MARK SUMNER

NEWS FROM THE EDGE: VAMPIRES OF VERMONT

An Ace Book / published by arrangement with
the author

PRINTING HISTORY
Ace edition / July 1999

Cover art by Jeffrey Walker.

For information address: The Berkley Publishing Group,
a division of Penguin Putnam Inc.,
375 Hudson Street, New York, New York 10014.

The Penguin Putnam Inc. World Wide Web site address is
http://www.penguinputnam.com

Check out the Ace Science Fiction/Fantasy newsletter,
and much more, at Club PPI!

ISBN: 0-441-00628-0

ACE®
Ace Books are published by The Berkley Publishing Group,
a division of Penguin Putnam Inc.,
375 Hudson Street, New York, New York 10014.
ACE and the "A" design are trademarks
belonging to Penguin Putnam Inc.

PRINTED IN THE UNITED STATES OF AMERICA

10 9 8 7 6 5 4 3 2 1

"COUNT DRACULA'S ON LINE TWO, AND HE SOUNDS pissed."

I raised my head from my desk and peered out through my tangled hair. I was on the tail end of a week-long bout with the flu, and I felt about as effective as a snot-soggy Kleenex and looked even less attractive. The sight of Caroline March looming over my desk with her sleek Donna Karan suit and impeccably stylish blond coif did nothing to improve my disposition.

Caroline mimed holding a phone to her head. "Excuse me, Ms. McKinnon, there's a blood-drinking dweeb on the cold-call line." She spoke slowly, as if explaining the function of a light switch to a two-year-old. "*Tu comprendo* fang face on the phone?"

"You mean Count Yorga?" I asked, my voice little better than a croak.

"Oh no," Caroline replied. "I'm talking about the other lunatic that thinks he's a vampire and calls you every day.'' She let out an exasperated sigh. ''Of *course* I mean that creep called Yorga.''

Compared to most of my conversations with Caroline, this was a civil beginning. I blinked my blurry eyes and sat up straighter in my seat. ''What's wrong?''

Caroline folded her bright red fingernails along the smooth blue sleeves of her jacket and pressed her lips flat in a show of disdain. Disdain was the cornerstone of Caroline's personality. ''How should I know, Ms. famous reporter McKinnon? He's your pet loon.''

''He's not crazy.'' I pushed my rebellious hair back from my face and tried to settle my cracked voice.

''He's certifiable.'' Caroline looked down at me and rolled her eyes. ''But then, I suppose from your point of view he doesn't look that bad.''

Her words echoed in my cough-syrup-saturated mind. I was too woozy to sort out all the inferences, but I was pretty sure I had been insulted. From my first day at the *Global Query*, Caroline had treated me as if I were the junior assistant copygirl. Somehow she seemed to feel that her stories—the majority of which concerned the unlikely, and usually unsavory, dating habits of middle-aged celebrities—were far more important than the columns that went out under my byline.

''Count Yorga is the primary source for an ongoing series of articles,'' I said. I tried to pack as much dignity as I could into the words.

Caroline snorted. ''Only you would call this nutcase a source. Do you honestly think this fruit loop is really a vampire?''

All around the newsroom, faces turned away from the pale glow of monitors. The clatter of fingers on keyboards fell away. The hum of conversation ceased. It was suddenly quiet—too quiet. My coworkers might not have been the sharpest collection of journalists ever crammed into one sleazy tabloid, but they could still catch a hint of blood in the water. My ongoing war with Ms. March had been a principle source of entertainment around the newsroom for months.

I rubbed at my gummy eyes and cleared my throat. On an average day, I felt more than able to handle Caroline in a battle of wits—after all, she was packing low-caliber mental ammunition—but my flu had left me feeling completely unarmed. Besides, my feelings about this particular source matched Caroline's position more closely than I was willing to admit.

"Well . . ." I answered carefully. "Count Yorga displays a very vivid imagination."

Caroline laughed. Maybe it was just me, but I found her laughter about as pleasant as a dentist's drill being dragged across a blackboard. "Let me put it in terms you'll understand: Your Count Yorga is at least two McNuggets short of a Happy Meal."

"No, he's not. . . ."

"Oh, please." The sarcasm in Caroline's voice was so thick you could have used it on pancakes. "Your friend the vampire is playing hockey with a warped puck and you're turning his psychoses into stories."

A whisper ran through the newsroom. I could almost hear the scorecards being marked to show another goal for Caroline.

Men and women leaned forward in their chairs as they awaited my riposte. The faces of our colleagues looked toward us with the eager expression of the crowd at a boxing match. I sucked in a deep breath and tried to think of which way to jab. Her article on Madonna's silver-plated nursing bras? Her interview with Ross Perot's secret love child?

Instead I let my breath out through my teeth. I was in no condition to brawl. I ran my fingers through my tangled hair and summoned up my best mock smile. "Thanks for bringing the call to my attention, Caroline," I said, my saccharine tone only slightly roughened by my tangle with a virus. "I'll check it out right away."

There was a moment of shocked silence. Then a disappointed rumble passed through the newsroom as people realized I wasn't going to return fire. One by one my coworkers turned away. Gradually, the sounds of typing and talking returned.

Caroline didn't rebound quite so quickly. For a good thirty seconds she stood beside my desk with a puzzled expression on her thin, coldly pretty face. Finally she seemed to get the idea that I really was not going to play. "Well," she said in an uncertain tone. "Next time answer your own phone calls."

Count Yorga's calls always came in through the general outside line. I wasn't certain how I was supposed to screen calls that didn't come to my number, but I wasn't about to say anything that might give Caroline a reason to stay. "I'll try," I offered.

With a final glare, Caroline spun and walked away. My artificial smile slipped as she went out of sight. I gave my weary nose a quick blow, grimaced at the flashing light on my phone, and reached toward the receiver with considerable reluctance.

"This is Savvy Skye," I said. At least I managed to remember my *nom de plume.* So far as the readers of the *Query* knew, I was Savvy Skye, ace reporter of all things strange, bizarre, and downright weird, not Savannah McKinnon, frustrated journalist stuck in a dead-end job with the country's sleaziest tabloid.

For a moment there was only buzzing static on the other end of the phone line. The noise soared up into a squawk, followed by a quick series of rising squeaks. I pulled the phone away from my ear and stared at it. ''Hello?'' I called, my lips several inches clear of the mouthpiece.

A series of sharp trills came from the phone, then a solid click—like a man clucking his tongue against the roof of his mouth. ''I don't like to be kept waiting, Ms. Skye,'' said a faint voice that was laced with a heavy accent.

I quickly pressed the phone to my ear. ''I'm sorry. I guess the phone system around here isn't everything it could be.''

''Is that so?'' There was a rattle, and a rusty wheezing from the other end of the phone. This was a familiar sound. My last two conversations with my ''vampire'' caller had been marked by long pauses and these unsteady gasps for breath. Yorga wouldn't give a location, and the *Query*'s caller ID system drew a blank when it came to locating his phone, but I was beginning to wonder if my would-be bloodsucker was phoning in his tales of night stalking from a bed at some hospital or nursing home.

''Are you all right?'' I asked.

''Certainly,'' he replied in a choked voice. The statement was followed by a dry, rattling cough. ''Count Yorga is eternal.''

He didn't sound eternal. In fact, his voice sounded much worse than it had the last time we talked. His accent was the same as ever—an unlikely mixture of Bela Lugosi and William F. Buckley Jr.—but the coarse, sandpapery texture of his words was new. Listening to the count struggle made my little tussle with the flu seem not nearly so serious.

One of Caroline's jibes resurfaced in my histamine-clouded mind. The count had been calling for almost a month, and his eccentric ramblings had generated a good string of articles—very popular articles, according to the number-grinding automatons down in marketing. But if my vampire was actually suffering from some progressive illness or serious mental imbalance, I might really be guilty of making money off his misery. Writing for a tabloid was never the best way to improve your moral standing, but I did have some limits.

"Mister—I mean *Count* Yorga," I said, "are you sure everything is all—"

Before I could finish, there was a growl from the other end of the phone. "No, everything is not all right!" The count roared with surprising force.

"I thought you just said that you were—"

"I am fine," Yorga snapped, cutting me off again. "It is you who is far from all right."

For a moment I felt a spike of fear. It was true that I had been under the weather—more like six feet under—but Yorga had no way of knowing I'd been ill. The count's statement raised the distinctly unsettling idea that he might actually be spying on me in some way. In the last six months, I'd had several bits of fan mail that edged over the line into the moderately chillifying. So far, none of it had led to anything, but I couldn't be sure that happy state would continue. The readership of the *Query* was strange enough; the idea of one of our contributors setting his sights on me was enough to make me regret not taking a promising position as a domestic servant or a fast-food supervisor. Just what I needed: a stalker that thought he was a vampire.

I picked my words carefully. "What do you think is wrong with me?" For a moment, I had a terrible fear that the voice on the phone was going to mention something personal—something about my hair, or my dress. Something about the way I had looked when I trudged out of my apartment that morning.

The count ended my speculation quickly. "I do not think," he said. "I know. You have misquoted me."

I let out a trembling breath. Okay, for the moment it didn't look like the count was spending his imagined immortality peeking through my mail slot. Making mistakes in a quote was clearly a journalistic no-no, but I'd certainly take that kind of criticism over being followed by someone with porcelain fangs.

"I never misquoted—" I began.

"You did!" Yorga snapped. "You—" His words were cut off by a fit of coughing. When he continued, his voice was back to a more normal tone. "You altered my words."

I stood up, stretched the phone cord to its limits, and managed to snag the latest issue of the *Global Query* from a neighboring cubicle. The cover showed a large photo of a fry cook kneeling in awe before a grilled cheese sandwich marked with the image of Jesus and the Apostle Peter. Crowding the miracle sandwich on the right was an article on the healing powers of cilantro and another on psychic predictions for the new television season. Wedged in the corner of the page was a toothy shot of a vampire with its mouth gaping open and eyes blazing red. Inch-high letters accompanied the shot.

VAMPIRE COUNT SPILLS BLOODY
SECRETS OF THE UNDEAD

I flipped through the issue to the third page where the rest of my article on Yorga continued under the glare of another stock vampire shot. It was a relatively long article, three columns of small text that left no room for anything on the page but an ad for copper arthritis bracelets. I scanned the columns quickly.

"The story seems to be in order," I said. "I don't see anything wrong."

"Of course you don't," Yorga snarled. "I doubt that anyone with your distinct lack of journalistic skill would spot a whale in a bathtub."

It was time to do a little snarling of my own. I had already surrendered one fight to Caroline; I was in no hurry to lose another. "Now listen, Mr. Yorga—"

"It's *Count* Yorga," he interrupted before I could get my rant off the ground. "And you misquoted me three times. Three times!"

I ground my teeth together, pinned the phone against my shoulder and scowled down at the article. "Where?" I asked.

There was the sound of rustling paper on the other end of the phone. "Here, you imbecile," said the count. "Right here in the first paragraph where I told you my age."

I traced my finger along the column and speared the sentence in question. "I see it. You told me you were over four hundred years old."

"No!" the vampire roared. "I said 'four hundred and twelve'."

"Four hundred and twelve is over four hundred," I said with as much patience as I could muster.

"Pre—" started Yorga, but before he could finish a word, he fell into another bout of dry, whistling coughs. "Precision," he said when the storm abated. "There's a total lack of precision. What you wrote was not a quote."

I squirmed a little uncomfortably in my chair. "It contained the essence of your statement."

"The essence," Yorga repeated. His sarcasm level made Caroline's jabs seem like praise. "What about here in the next paragraph, where you have me saying I'm from Germany?"

I nodded at the unseeing phone. "That is what you said."

"Wrong," he shot back. "I said I was born in Prussia, not Germany!"

"But Prussia is part of Germany today."

"It's not a quote . . . it's a . . . it's—" He broke off in another fit of coughing. "It's only a summary."

"Look, Mr. Yorga, some of your statements were rather long," I said as patiently as I could manage. "We only have so much space in the paper. Not everything can make the final cut."

"Idiot!" bellowed the count. An enormous sigh rattled through the phone line. "Enough of this," he said. "Let me speak to the editor in charge."

I closed my eyes. Calling Mr. Genovese in to handle a flipped out vampire was not likely to be a great career move. "Look, Mr. Yorga—"

"Count!" he screamed into the phone with such force

that I could hear spit sizzling against the mouthpiece. "Can't you even get that much right? Get me that editor or the next reporter I talk to will be at the *Weekly World News*!"

At the sound of those words, I felt a thrill more terrifying than the thought of any vampire. The *Weekly World News*. There might be a hundred monsters on the pages of the *Global Query*, but there was only one beast that made a regular appearance in our newsroom. The *Weekly* consistently beat out the *Query* in the numbers and in the pure outrageousness of its headlines. Mr. Genovese could often be found growling at an issue of the *News* whenever our own front page seemed particularly lame.

Yorga might be a nutball, but he had found the one threat that would make me listen. "You don't want to go to them," I said quickly. "You think I've made mistakes, you just let those butchers at the *News* get—"

"Enough! The editor, or I walk."

I was tempted to mention that the count's European accent had faded under stress, but I fought that temptation away quickly. "Hold on. I'll get Mr. Genovese." I tapped the hold button, then spent a few seconds staring at the silent handset. Somehow I didn't think serious reporters let themselves be bullied by their sources. Especially sources with fangs.

"This is going to be so much fun," I mumbled. Suddenly my throat seemed very sore and my head very heavy. I transferred the call to Mr. Genovese and dropped the phone back into the cradle. Then I sat back to wait for the explosion.

It took longer than I expected. I was almost ready to slip out for lunch when the door at the far end of the newsroom banged open and a voice bellowed over the cubicles. ‘‘Ms. McKinnon! In the office. Now.’’

I stood, ran my fingers across my rumpled dress, and walked down the narrow aisles of the newsroom with a brand of gallows-bound resignation. My head was swimming with so much decongestant that the dusty tile floor pitched like the deck of the HMS *Bounty* rounding Cape Horn. I staggered into the editor’s office with one hand on the door frame for support.

Bill Genovese, part owner and sole editor of the *Global Query,* stood with his face turned down and his big hands gripping the edge of his desk top. There was a copy of the *Query* spread out on the desk. Even from across the room I could see it was open to one of my transcripts of Count Yorga’s diatribes.

I cleared my throat and braced myself. ‘‘You wanted to see me?’’

Mr. Genovese looked up from the paper. Right away, the expression on his face let me know I was in big, big trouble. He was smiling. This was a situation so rare it was nearly unprecedented. A smile on Bill Genovese’s face looks about as natural as Pamela Lee’s bustline. I had absolutely no doubt that I was in for a really bad day.

‘‘Your vampire pal is royally pissed about the misquotes,’’ he said. The smile faded as he talked, but the man still looked disturbingly cheerful.

‘‘That’s what I hear.’’ I licked at my cracked lips. ‘‘But it wasn’t misquotes,’’ I insisted, ‘‘just summarization.’’

Mr. Genovese shook his head. ‘‘If it goes in quotes, it had better be quotes.’’

I was too stunned to reply. First Bill Genovese had

actually smiled at me, now I was getting lectures on journalistic ethics from a man who regularly published articles on the contents of celebrity garbage bins. I had entered the tabloid *Twilight Zone.*

Mr. Genovese grabbed the edge of the paper on his desk and spun it around to face me. The center of the page featured an especially toothsome vampire looming behind an unsuspecting woman in a tight sweater. I recognized the woman as one of the assistants from the front office. The *Query* did not hesitate when it came to using the office staff as props.

The editor stabbed a thick finger against the vampire's snarling face. "What's your opinion of this series, Ms. McKinnon?"

I took a step closer and shrugged. "They're . . . all right," I said.

"Is that all?"

I wrinkled my nose. The stories were nonsense, but they were nonsense with my byline attached. I felt compelled to provide at least a bare minimum of support. "Yorga's stories are entertaining, and they have a lot of details."

"Details." Mr. Genovese shook his head and the smile disappeared from his face. It was quickly replaced by his usual scowl. "Yorga's stories are derivative crap that skims from every B horror flick in the last fifty years."

In a strange way, the sour expression and sharp words made me feel better. "Well, yes, but—"

I was cut off with a wave of a beefy hand. "Anyway, that's not important." He reached to the desk top and picked up a yellow sheet of paper packed with tight rows of tiny numbers. "What's important is that the marketing department rates this series as one of the most popular in the last six months. This vampire crap really pulls the eyeballs.''

Eyeballs. There was an image I could have done without. Marketing-speak always seemed a little on the slimy side. ''Are the numbers really that good?'' I asked.

''Not great,'' the editor replied, ''but they've gotten larger with every article.''

''Couldn't we just dig up something else? There's always another story.''

Mr. Genovese looked up from the papers. ''There's always another story,'' he agreed, ''but when you're being handed material that pulls in readers, you don't kick your source in his pointed teeth.'' No trace of the odd smile remained on his hard features and his words came out in short, firm barks. ''Is that clear, Ms. McKinnon?''

''Sure . . .'' I started. ''I mean, yes, sir.'' I considered adding a little salute, but thought that might be pushing it.

The editor nodded. ''Your Count Yorga is damn hot under the cape about being misquoted. He wants to take this story and give it to another paper.''

I winced. Even though the *Global Query* was about as far as you could get from mainstream journalism, Mr. Genovese retained an editor's instinctive hatred for losing any story to a rival. I nodded warily. ''I know. He made the same threat to me.''

''Then I'm sure you also know I'm not going to let that happen,'' said Mr. Genovese. ''Especially not when that other paper is the *Weekly World News.*'' He spat out the dreaded name as if it were laced with cyanide and rat turds, then he dropped into his chair and folded his arms across his barrel chest. ''Fortunately, the count and I were able to come to an agreement that will not only keep the story in our hands, but guarantee a surge in ratings.''

This was it. I could feel disaster hovering over me like a kind of reverse guardian angel. ''What kind of agreement?'' I asked.

Slowly the smile reformed on the editor's face. ''You're going to love it,'' he replied.

TWO

WHEN I WAS IN SIXTH GRADE, A GROWTH SPURT CATA-pulted me to a towering five foot three. For the space of nearly a school year, I was the tallest person in my class. Someone even nicknamed me Giraffe. Unfortunately, this surge of altitude turned out to be the high tide of my teenage hormones. I never gained another inch—at least not in height.

Since childhood, I had given up giraffedom to become a turtle, or maybe a miniature antelope. In any case, I had gotten used to being among the shortest people in almost any room. So it was something of a shock to step into the Greene County Lions Club Hall and discover that I had become a giant.

All around me a swarm of uniformed midgets milled and wrestled and bounced off the walls. The vast majority were blue-suited males, their pecking order laid out by neckerchiefs of varying shades and strings of badges. Scattered among them were a much smaller number of females, distinguished by their green coats and expressions of disgust.

Like an explorer stepping into a piranha-choked stream, I pushed carefully into the flow. Somewhere within this madhouse was Jimmy Knowles, currently editor of the minuscule weekly, the *Green County Journal,* and former foreign correspondent for the *Washington Post.* Jimmy and I had been bumping slowly down the long road from friendship to romance for months, and while Jimmy seemed happy enough to make this journey at glacial speed, I had some hopes that I could use the situation with Yorga to throw the relationship into overdrive. All I had to do was find Jimmy.

The jabbering horde gave way reluctantly, eyeing me from beneath the brims of their caps. I tried to remember the rules for such encounters. No sudden moves. Avoid contact. Don't look them directly in the eyes. I had penetrated only a few steps into the room when an unseen voice growled something in the unintelligible language of public address systems. At once the natives lost their interest in me. They turned, swirled, and drained away down a hallway, leaving me standing nearly alone in the hall.

I approached a solitary blue-suit who remained standing against the far wall, abandoned by the falling tide of scouts. "Hi," I said, smiling to show I was friendly.

Big brown eyes looked up at me. Without the support of his tribe, he seemed nearly paralyzed.

"Have you seen a man from the newspaper?" I asked.

There was a moment of consideration followed by a slow shake of a head.

"A guy from the *Green County Journal,*" I prompted hopefully. "He's supposed to be taking pictures."

With this additional bit of info, the brown eyes lit. "There's a girl," he said.

I spent a few seconds trying to make a connection between my question and his answer. "Not a girl," I said, shaking my head. "A man." I held my hand up about eight inches over my head. "About this tall. Brown hair with gray at the temples, lines around his eyes, but the good kind of lines, you know, not the . . . not . . ." My voice trailed away. The kid was looking at me with an expression that clearly said I might as well be speaking Swahili. I sighed. "Did you see a guy from the paper?"

"There's a girl," the kid repeated.

"Right, a girl." I flashed the lonely blue-suit a tired smile. "Thanks, you've been a big help." It was pretty clear that I had plumbed the depths of this resource. I turned away and decided to risk exploring the wild lion's den on my own.

A sprawling group of scouts had gathered around tables bearing orange soda and cookies. I weaved around this obstacle, dodged some strays making a run down the hall, ducked through a doorway, and stepped into the main hall just in time to be blinded by a photographer's flash. As the sparkles faded from my eyes, I found myself facing—a girl.

It appeared my one-sentence informer was correct about that much. She certainly was a girl.

She was young. Not as young as the scouts, but young enough to be wearing a sleeveless aqua T-shirt that left several inches of very flat stomach exposed above the concave waist of her very tight jeans—young enough to make my own twenty-five years feel more like a century. She had annoyingly thick auburn curls that were pulled back in a sickeningly cute ponytail behind a twist of ribbon. Her skin was atrociously clean and smooth, her face revoltingly beautiful, and the foulest, most despicable of her many ghastly crimes was the presence of Jimmy Knowles's strong hands on her bare, tan shoulders.

The small-town editor, former big-time newsman, and current candidate for a public hanging smiled as he guided the nymphet back. ''You might want to take a step away from the subject,'' said Jimmy. He pulled the tart away from a row of grinning scouts. ''And focus carefully. That old Mamiya doesn't give quite as much depth of field as you might think.''

The insidiously cute little vamp raised a battered black and chrome camera. ''Everybody hold still, okay?'' she called in a cheerful tone as she squinted through the lens. The scouts, of course, only squirmed more energetically—all except the older boys in the back row, who were staring at the girl with a species of awe. There was another flare from the camera and the mass of scouts scattered in all directions.

Jimmy took his hands from the tramp's shoulders. ''That was great, Jen,'' he said. He flashed a broad smile. ''You're a natural.''

''A natural what?'' I asked.

Jimmy's eyes flickered from the girl to me. I have to give him credit; his smile didn't waver for a moment. ''Savvy!'' he called cheerfully. ''Have you met Jen?''

''No, I don't think I have.'' I was suddenly and painfully aware of my less than optimum appearance. My hair and my makeup had both suffered neglect in the last few days. According to the Centers for Disease Control, this flu had come all the way from Australia just to make me come off bad in comparison to a girl photographer that looked like she should be in front of a camera instead of behind it. I decided to brave it out. I put a professional smile on my face, stepped toward this journalistic Lolita, and stretched out my hand.

The girl let the camera dangle from the strap around her neck and rushed to meet me. "Are you really Savvy Skye?" she asked breathlessly. Her all-too-blue eyes were wide, and her mouth actually gaped open in excitement.

"Savannah McKinnon," I replied. "Savvy Skye is just a pen name."

"But you're her, right? You're the one that writes all those stories in the *Global Query*?" She had yet to release my hand.

"That's me."

"Wow!" She spun to grin at Jimmy for a moment, dragging me forward a step in the process, then whirled back to me. "I mean, well . . . wow! You're like actually famous." She finally surrendered her death grip on my fingers and clamped her hands together with an air of supplication. Her expression had taken on something of the same quality I had seen in kindergartners at a Barney concert.

"I don't know about famous," I replied carefully. I certainly didn't think of my work at the *Query* as something to be particularly proud about. In fact, I often considered the whole rag to be a horrible waste of perfectly good pulpwood.

Jen seemed not to notice my lack of enthusiasm. She nodded with frantic zeal, sending her ponytail into a bouncy frenzy. "Sure you're famous. I bet a million people read your stories every week. I know I do." She leaned closer. "You know, some of the stories in the *Query* aren't very good." Her upturned nose wrinkled as she shared this brilliant bit of insight, then her smile beamed out brighter than ever. "But your articles are always really good. In fact, they're great!"

I knew at that moment that I had horribly misjudged a sweet and intelligent young student of journalism. The *Query* might be 99 percent pure crap, but Jen at least had an eye for the diamond of quality hidden in the endless miles of rough. "Thank you," I replied. "I really appreciate your candid observations."

Jen's smile, already broad enough to conjure bottomless dimples from beneath her high cheekbones, grew until it threatened to split her head in half. "Savvy Skye," she said. She shook her head in evident wonder. "You know, Mr. Knowles never stops talking about you."

I looked over at Jimmy and mentally canceled the mob hit I had been planning for him. "Doesn't he?"

"Yeah," Jen said, nodding again. "He says you could really be a major journalist. He says you've got—"

Jimmy touched the girl lightly on the arm. "Jen, how about putting away the camera gear while I talk to Ms. McKinnon?"

" 'Kay!" Jen spouted immediately. She gave me a final grin and turned away.

I shook my head as I watched her walk away. "You should have let her talk, the girl has some very important and perceptive observations."

"Uh-huh," replied Jimmy. "It looked like you were getting embarrassed."

"You can embarrass me with compliments all you want." I studied the amused expression in his blue-gray eyes. "If you coached her to say all those things, you did one hell of a job."

Jimmy's face fell under the heavy weight of questioned innocence. "Coached?" He leaned in and gave me a kiss. "Jen's just a fan of your work."

"Right." The kiss had been quick, but it was there. Bringing our relationship from friendship to something more had taken me months of careful, dedicated work. I had first gotten close to Jimmy in hopes of learning from his years of experience as an international journalist. Later, I became interested in . . . other areas of his knowledge. Now, looking down at my wrinkled clothes, I wished I had taken time to clean up before going in search of Jimmy. I didn't want to promote any backsliding.

"So, what does that child do when she's not busy being a Savvy Skye fan?" I asked.

Jimmy chuckled. "I believe she spends most of her time in high school, but starting this week, she's going to be doing about ten hours a week for the *Journal.*"

"Doing what?"

"Photography, manning the phone, whatever it takes." He shrugged. "Now that you're not volunteering so often, I needed to find some help."

I winced at that bit. For almost a year, I had done *gratis* work for Jimmy. Like most small-town local papers in these postliterate days, the *Green County Journal* was on a slow path to nonexistence. Readership was down and revenues could be measured in a stream of subscriptions that grew shallower each year. If Jimmy hadn't come along to buy the place, the *Journal* would have already been a memory.

Volunteering to scribble a few lines and glue together

a few pages at the *Journal* had earned me a measure of Jimmy's gratitude and allowed us to get closer, but over the last three months I had slipped away from working at the *Journal.* Part of that was an increase in my duties at the *Query,* but a bigger—and guiltier—part of my fading volunteerism was simple boredom. I mean, it was great to work alongside Jimmy, but after reporting on a dozen Weight Watchers meetings and two dozen PTO confrontations, I just wasn't as enthusiastic about the innate majesty of small-town news as I used to be. Working at the *Journal* did represent a certain level of respectability when compared to sleazing along at the *Query,* but I no longer believed it would help me scale that peak that lead to an anchor spot on the network news.

I glanced over my shoulder and watched Jen winding the film in the camera that was probably three times her age. "Can she write?" I asked.

Jimmy shrugged. "Her text style is a little rough, but she works hard at it. She's even been helping Shaver with the layout. . . ."

That last duty was enough to make me laugh. "You're forcing that poor girl to work on that decrepit printing equipment with Shaver Wilcox?" I shook my head. "He'll slice her up and spread her over the plates."

"You'd be surprised," Jimmy replied. "Jen and Shaver have really hit it off."

"They have?" I turned and watched Jen as she put the camera and flash bars back into their cases. The girl might be a fan, but she still bore careful watching. Shaver Wilcox was the crankiest, sourest old man I had ever met. Anyone that could charm Shaver was definitely dangerous. "Are you sure this girl is only there to help out with the paper?"

"What do you mean?"

I scowled at him and nodded across the room to where the red-haired Jen was still packing away gear. "Somehow I suspect there were plenty of students in this town that would like to work at the paper. What makes me think this girl got the position for more than her journalism grades?"

The comment brought a grin to Jimmy's face. "You're already twenty years too young for me. If I started anything with Jen they'd throw me under the jail."

"The age of consent is sixteen in Missouri."

"Is it?" Jimmy raised an eyebrow and turned slowly toward Jen. "Well, then . . ."

"Jimmy!"

He laughed and spun back to me. "I'm kidding," he said. "Don't kill me." He leaned down and gave me a quick kiss on the cheek. "Hey, what brings you over here? I thought you were home sick."

I shrugged. "I was, but I had to go in before Mr. Genovese fired me."

Jimmy grinned. "Don't let Bill play any mind games with you. You're too good a writer for him to let you go. If you're sick, get some rest."

"I'm not sick, I'm . . . I'm . . ." As if summoned by the mere mention of my waning flu, a massive sneeze began to build. I fumbled open my purse and grabbed for the wrinkled mass of tissue just in time to stop the majority of the spray. "I'm not sick," I restated, wiping away the results of the explosion. "I'm feeling much better."

Jimmy nodded. ''Oh, absolutely. I can see that you're ready to party all night and work all day.''

''I am!'' I fought back a sniff. ''In fact, I came here to see if you wanted to get away for the weekend.''

I had hoped for excitement; what I got was a frown. ''The weekend? I'm not sure, Savvy. There's an awful lot to do at the *Journal.*''

''There's always a lot to do at the *Journal.*'' I made a surreptitious check to see that my fingers were free of snot, then reached out to take Jimmy's hand. ''Come on, this could be a great chance to move our relationship past trips to the movies and two dinners a week.''

He considered the proposal. And considered. This was bad. Any man who wanted to spend a weekend with his girlfriend did not frown at the prospect.

Instead of giving me a straight yes or no, Jimmy tacked hard to starboard. ''Where are you going?'' he asked. ''Hunting yeti? Sneaking into Area 51?''

I tried to keep my smile in place as I dropped the other half of the proposal. ''Actually, I was thinking Vermont.''

''And what's in Vermont?''

''Um . . . a vampire.''

Twenty-five years of covering the news had given Jimmy an admirable ability to roll with the punches. He barely raised an eyebrow. ''Vampire?''

I quickly outlined the background of the vampire count and his increasingly frequent calls to the paper. ''So now Mr. Genovese wants me to patch things up with the count by doing a face-to-face interview. He's promised Yorga the front page.''

Jimmy nodded. ''Of course he has. I can see the headline now.'' He raised his hands with the tips of his thumbs pressed together and his fingers held upwards, like a make-believe movie director framing a shot. "INTERVIEW WITH THE VAMPIRE."

I winced, but nodded. "Exactly."

"You'll be lucky if you're not sued. Anne Rice will probably be running the paper by next Thursday."

"We're sued every week," I replied with a shrug. "Mr. Genovese thinks it will sell papers."

Jimmy sighed. "I'm sure he's right." A sad expression tightened the corners of his mouth. "Too bad Bill didn't think of running something really unusual—like actual news."

I licked my lips and tried not to seem too eager. "If you come along, maybe you could help me find some real news."

"Savvy," Jimmy said with a shake of his head. "I don't even think you're ready for this trip."

"Not ready?" I felt the first red stirrings of anger and disappointment. I might take insults from my collegues at the *Query,* but Jimmy's opinion really mattered to me. "You think I can't handle a field assignment?"

"It's not that," Jimmy said quickly. "It's only that you've been sick for a couple of weeks. Instead of going out into the snow and making yourself worse, you need to stay home and rest."

Another sneeze began to surface. I stifled it brutally, turning it into an internal squeak that threatened to rupture my eardrums. "I'm fine," I said around what I hoped was a confident smile. "I can wrap up this story in an hour, then you and I can have a whole weekend to knock around New England." I put my hand on his arm. "If I get feeling too bad, I'm sure you can take care of me."

Jimmy stared straight into my eyes for a moment, then looked away. "I just don't think it's a good idea for us to go up there together, Savvy."

A more cautious person might have cut her losses at this point. I could have nodded, kissed Jimmy on the cheek, and still come back to a relationship of movie dates and lunchtime chats. But I was tired of being cautious. "Why not?" I asked. "We've been going out for months now. Don't you think it's time to move this relationship forward?"

The pained expression on Jimmy's face became even stronger. "To be honest, Savvy, I've been thinking it was time to move it backwards."

Sharp little pains started jabbing into my temples and I could feel my pulse pounding in my throat. "What does that mean?"

Jimmy reached out and took both my hands in his. He glanced around for a moment, and when he spoke again he lowered his voice to a near whisper. "Savvy, I think you're extraordinary," he said. "You're intelligent. You're funny. You're talented." He paused for a second and smiled. "And it doesn't hurt that you're gorgeous."

Ordinarily, I was highly susceptible to this kind of flattery—even if it wasn't true. But on this occasion, I could sense that Jimmy's pleasing words were only the prelude to disaster.

"But . . ." I prompted.

Jimmy sighed. "But you're younger than my daughter," he said. "I should never have let this get started."

I closed my eyes and tried to think, but that acid mix of anger and frustration was rising up through me like the mercury in a thermometer held against a radiator.

The age thing. It was always Jimmy's trump card. Every time we started to get really close, he tossed it on the table. By the time I opened my eyes, I had sorted out my emotions.

I was going with anger.

"Why don't you tell me the truth, Jimmy?" I demanded, pulling my hands from his grip.

Jimmy shook his head. "I just—"

"No," I cut in. "You gave me an excuse." I stepped forward so quickly that he stumbled a step back. "If you really thought I was as great as you say, you wouldn't let a few years come between us."

The expression on Jimmy's face might have been fear, might have been guilt. It was definitely not good. "Savvy, you know I care about you. But it's not a few years. It's—"

I interrupted him again. I believe I made some sort of growl. Maybe something closer to a scream. Whatever it was, when I turned around I found an audience of Jen and a dozen Boy Scouts. All of them appeared to be frozen in shock.

There didn't seem to be anything left to say—or snarl. Without another glance at Jimmy, I stomped off for the exit. At every step, my anger dropped ten degrees, but my heart continued to beat somewhere in the vicinity of my chin. A whole year working on this relationship—moving from coworkers, to friends, to . . . to . . . to what? We had barely passed the passion level of a G movie. My first date as a teenager had held more kisses than Jimmy had delivered total. I had been an idiot to carry this on for so long. Jimmy was right; I was twenty years younger than he was. I could find another guy.

Someone my own age. Someone who was really interested in me.

I stopped at the door and leaned against the frame. ‘‘Jimmy,’’ I whispered.

‘‘Um, Savvy?’’

I turned around to see Jen standing in the hall behind me with a painfully cute expression of concern on her pretty face. ‘‘What is it?’’ I asked. My voice sounded rough and raw.

‘‘You really like him, huh?’’ asked the teenager.

I started to shake my head, but shrugged instead. ‘‘Does it matter? He doesn’t like me the same way.’’

Jen bit her full lower lip, glanced over her shoulder for a second, then looked back at me. ‘‘There was this guy at school that was chasing me for a whole semester. He asked me out on a date every single weekend, but I said no.’’

‘‘That’s great,’’ I replied. ‘‘Is there a point to this?’’ Having Jen’s abundant adolescent love life shoved in my face didn’t seem like a good therapeutic strategy.

The girl nodded. ‘‘This guy, he finally stopped asking me out. And you know what?’’

I sighed. ‘‘What?’’

‘‘I missed him,’’ said Jen. She leaned toward me and lowered her voice. ‘‘Now I’m chasing him.’’

A few seconds cranked slowly past while I tried to make sense of what she was telling me. ‘‘You think Jimmy will—?’’

Jen nodded, her ponytail keeping time. ‘‘He really likes you. Wait and see.’’ With that, she turned and headed back into the building.

I stood in the doorway for at least a minute before stepping into the cold outside air. Maybe Jen was right.

Maybe pushing Jimmy away was just what our relationship needed to move on. Let him see that I was not always going to be there. Make him value me a little more.

On the other hand, he might be inside breathing a sigh of relief. Maybe he wouldn't miss me at all.

When you start taking advice on your relationships from teenagers who wear bare-midriff tops in the middle of the winter, the bottom of the barrel cannot be far away.

THE GUY IN THE NEXT SEAT WEIGHED AT LEAST A HUNdred pounds more than the plane designers had anticipated when they built the seats. Wedges of fat were jammed in under the armrests and his shoulders were on my side of the divide. The guy had a shiny bald spot on his basketball-sized head, thick glasses on his potato-shaped nose, and really bad taste in suits. Still, I was jealous. No matter what this guy had going against him, he had one big thing going for him: he could sleep on planes.

I stared at him with undiluted envy. Despite taking a handful of antihistamines to ward off any resurgence of the Cold from Hell, I could not achieve the state of blessed unconsciousness I so desperately craved. Any attempt I made at closing my eyes left me with feelings of falling, which were soon followed by stomach-boiling panic that jolted me back to sweaty alertness. Compound these unpleasant sensations with thoughts of Jimmy whenever I was awake, and it was a recipe designed to keep me staring at the headrest in front of me all morning. The fat man was obviously unafflicted with these problems. He was snoozing before we were off the ground in St. Louis, a tiny airline pillow jammed at the back of his neck.

It was hard to blame him. The red-eye flight to Boston was supposed to slip out of the airport around midnight, but given a dose of bad weather topped off with a few mystical airline delays, we didn't actually roll off the tarmac until almost six A.M. Anyone that could sleep was sleeping. That left me and two bored flight attendants to stare out the windows as dawn painted red streaks along the crumpled tops of clouds. It was certainly beautiful—cotton-candy pink, shimmering gold, an orange to make oranges green with envy—but I would have traded the sight in a second for three hours of solid sleep.

My discomfort at being awake was not aided by my wardrobe. A lot of people treat air travel like it's an occasion demanding semiformal attire. Not me. My usual airliner outfit is either sweats too loose to wear at the health club or a dress with roughly the same contours as a hefty bag. Either way, "comfort" is the operative word. But on this particular trip, I was betrayed by fluctuations in my ever-elastic measurements. As part of my campaign to capture Jimmy's affections, I had resorted to exercise—two months of daily visits to that heartless beast known as a StairMaster. Follow that up with two weeks of flu, and the combination generates enough weight loss to put Jenny Craig out of business. Half the poundage would probably return after a few decent meals, but for the moment I found myself flirting with my first size six since junior high. Unfortunately, flirting was all I was doing. All those miles of stairs had done their work at trimming my thighs, but my nether regions were still a solid size eight. If only I had kept that reality firmly in mind while picking my wardrobe for this assigment. A thousand miles in undersized jeans was definitely not a situation conducive to comfort.

By the time the plane arced over the breakfasting citizens of Ohio, even one of the attendants was snoring in her seat. At that point, I had further stressed my taut trousers by munching on the two bags of mini pretzels that passed for an airline meal. I squirmed in my seat for another half an hour until I had exhausted the dubious pleasures of browsing the overpriced catalog jammed into the seat pocket. Finally, more to take my mind off the permanent groove being carved in my midsection than from any real interest in the story, I fumbled open my bag and pulled out the file on Yorga.

It wasn't a very thick file. The *Global Query*'s favorite bloodsucker had only been phoning home for a little over a month. In the early calls the conversations had been brief—he was usually off the phone before I could get out more than a couple of questions. Still, scanning those early paragraphs, I could see the start of a pattern that Yorga would follow in later conversations—an affection for celebrity. Our count was quite the namedropper. But where a typical *Query* caller might claim to have the dirt on Arnold, Cindy, or Demi, Yorga's accounts featured even more famous names. His reminiscences of the past four centuries were liberally sprinkled with mentions of presidents, captains of industry, and other notables. According to the self-styled count, he had been around for the founding of the nation, handy for half the battles in the Civil War, and close at hand for every event from Woodstock to Watergate.

Of course, it was all nonsense. Even if I was to consider the extremely unlikely idea that vampires might actually exist, and even if these part-time bats could hang by their toes for hundreds of years, there was still a big problem with the story Yorga told. Problems, actually.

I was no great expert on history, but even I could tell that several of the count's anecdotes were as truthful as the average episode of Jerry Springer. Newton was not holding any conversations in 1795 and Lincoln wasn't giving speeches in 1878—at least not in this universe. Similarly, the vampire's memoirs often found historical figures cavorting in places they had never visited during their lives.

For someone that became so angry over my changing a few details in his quotes, Yorga didn't seem to be bothered by these inconsistencies in the source material. The inaccuracies of dates and places continued straight through all of Yorga's quotes—right up to a mention of John F. Kennedy at a date that would have made the late president twenty years older than his birth certificate.

After scanning the whole mess it became clear that, despite the warped history book worth of big names and bad dates, Count Yorga's personal tale was still full of century-wide gaps. It looked like I had plenty of ground to cover during Mr. Genovese's publicity stunt. There was no mention of how Yorga had started his life as a vampire, and little note of the first two hundred years of his undeath. Those were details that were sure to interest the *Query*'s readers. Regardless of the sheer silliness of the whole affair, I pulled out a legal pad and began to scribble some potential questions for the upcoming interview.

I wrote one pointed inquiry, then another, and was actually feeling fairly pleased with myself. Then I put the pencil down a minute and closed my eyes to think. When I opened them, I noticed that my surroundings had made an abrupt and unexpected change.

Instead of the window seat of a 737, I found myself parked in a purple wingback chair in front of a small mahogany table. I tried to blink away a dizzying wave of disorientation, but the world remained a little blurry at the edges. Around me the darkened room was filled with vague, twisted shadows and whispered voices that lingered in the air. A single candle burned fitfully on a silver plate at the center of the table, its bobbing flame stirring the shadows around me into tenebrous life. The fat man in the neighboring seat, the sleepy flight attendants, and all the others that had slogged aboard the delayed plane were gone. Within the shifting circle of candlelight I was all alone.

I stood up from the padded chair and squinted into the darkness. One corner of my brain was trying hard to deliver a message that the situation was way, way off track. Airplanes did not have little tables and shadowy rooms—not even when you were on your way to meet a vampire. But the rest of my mind was busy trying to peer into the darkness.

"Hello?" I called.

There was no answer. I tried to take a step, but the floor was oddly soft and spongy under my feet. "Hello?" I tried again. "Is anyone there?"

There was a dry, skittering sound like leaves blowing along a sidewalk or the last faint echo of laughter.

I pulled one foot free from the sagging floor and ventured another step. "Is anyone out there?"

The sound came again. This time it was followed by a swirl of movement from across the room. A tall shadow dislodged itself from the surrounding darkness. I could just make out the round shape of a head, and the broad reach of shoulders.

"Jimmy?" I asked in a choked, hopeful whisper.

"No," the black-on-black shape replied, matching my whisper. "Not Jimmy."

I moved as quickly as the rubbery floor would allow to put the chair between myself and the advancing figure. I looked around wildly. Surely this room had to have a door somewhere in the darkness. "Who are you?" I asked.

"Who were you looking for?" asked the dry voice. The shape came closer, moving toward the table and the dim glow of the candle. "Why did you leave your home?"

I took a step back and found my shoulder blades wedged against an unseen wall that felt warm and yeilding. "An interview," I said. There was a tremble in my voice, but I swallowed it down. "I came to see one of my sources."

"Yes, that's right." Long, dead white fingers slipped out of the shadows and grasped the candle. The yellow cone of fire at the candle's end began to grow brighter. "You're here for *Yorga.*" The name was a dry hiss.

I nodded dumbly. "Are you—"

"Yorga the ancient," interrupted the hard, cold voice. The candle abruptly flared, filling in the shadows with harsh, pale light. The sudden brutal glare revealed a towering skeletal figure draped in the torn remains of a silken cape. "Yorga!" cried the voice at a suddenly gut-wobbling volume. "Yorga the vampire!"

There was a final burst of white light. In that blaze I saw a face like the muzzle of some awful bleached beast fixed with a double pair of fangs. The skin was blue-white, the mouth a lipless wound set with the huge, glistening teeth. A leaden paralysis swept my body as the awful grinning face came closer. Closer. Blood dripped from the tips of the fangs as the vampire leaned in for the kill.

"Excuse me, miss?" said a voice at my ear.

I jumped and opened my eyes. The fat man was looking at me with concern, his eyes magnified by round-framed glasses. Behind him rows of empty airline seats stretched toward the front of the cabin and scalding morning light streamed in through a string of round-shouldered windows. A few remaining people in business suits and puffy winter coats were slowly filing out along the airplane's narrow aisle.

"You okay?" asked my worried neighbor.

"Uh, yeah." Liar. "Absolutely." Not. "Just fine." Except that my heart was racing like a hummingbird after a double expresso. I blinked against the glare from the windows and squinted at the passing people. There didn't seem to be any snake-jawed vampires in the immediate vicinity. "Where are we?" I asked. This time there was no disguising the tremble of lingering fear in my voice.

"Boston," the man replied. "Are you sure you're all right? It sounded like you were having a nightmare."

"I'm fine." I rubbed my tired eyes and shivered. The vision of that dark room with its single candle and fanged occupant still lingered in my head.

"Well, okay," said the man. He pushed his bulk out of his seat, then turned back to me. "Uh, maybe you should sit down somewhere, get a cup of coffee. I'd be happy to stay with you until you feel better."

Now I had something new to be afraid of. I shook my head. "No, that's okay."

"My treat."

"Thanks, but no," I replied. I unbuckled my seat belt and stood up. My head just brushed the top of the overhanging luggage rack—one of the few times when it was good to be short. "I really need to get going."

The overweight man looked disappointed, and he continued to cast hopeful glances my way as we grabbed our bags and shuffled from the plane. Once we were in the airport, I put on a burst of speed and soon left my would-be suitor behind.

I ran my fingers through my tangled hair. There wasn't a mirror in sight, but I could tell I had a serious case of airplane hair. Even without Jimmy, I couldn't wait till I could get to the Stone River Inn in Williams Crossing, Vermont. I might not be able to follow through on my original plans for a romantic weekend, but at least I could change out of the tight jeans, take a good shower, and catch some sleep.

Unfortunately, the national transportation system continued to conspire to keep me from my destination. First there were the usual thousand and one gates between me and the main terminal. Then I stood in the external and semiendless line waiting for a rental car. Then there was more wait for the van to take me to the car lot. By the time I was actually behind the wheel of what passed for a mid-sized car, almost two hours had passed. Noon had come and gone, and I still had miles to go before I could unbutton my jeans and get some rest.

Boston traffic was, well—Boston traffic. I spent another hour waiting out traffic jams under the green metal ramps of the highways while red-and-white commuter trains outpaced us along their rails.

Several times I felt drowsiness lurking near as I sat on the gridlocked interstate, but before I could nod off at the wheel a vision of white skin and a fang-filled mouth would send me back to shivering alertness. The dream of Yorga was absolutely ridiculous, but that didn't keep me from shivering.

When I wasn't alternating between sleep and fear, I took time to glance around at my surroundings. I spotted several places where I had stayed, eaten, or visited back in college. It had only been a couple of years since I had been an undergrad working on a college paper right there in the Boston area—a fact that seemed more incredible than anything printed in the tabloids. Back then, I had my future all planned out—a stint with a major daily, a little time with NPR to polish my credibility, then off to the network. The way I figured it, I would be behind an anchor desk by thirty. Somehow, reality had not quite conformed to those expectations. If I was going to get behind that desk, things were going to have to start moving awfully soon. I felt absolutely no compulsion to rush over to the campus and tell any of my professors about my position with the *Global Query.*

Finally, traffic began to fragment and I rolled away from the core of the city. The Boston area might be familiar to me from my college days, but as a student I had never felt a need to launch myself into the untracked wilderness that lay north and west of the sprawling suburbs. Now that I was there, I found it a little disappointing. Mainly because the wilderness just wasn't very wild. Even in the places where there was countryside, I found it a peculiarly civilized form of country. There were no great stretches that weren't liberally sprinkled with snug, often large, homes. Freshly painted barns backed up many of the multistory houses, but most of those had the appearance of something that was intended as a decorative statement, not a working farm. There was no doubt the area was pretty, but it also had a distinctly artificial air when compared to the more ragged countryside in the center of the nation. It wasn't aided by the fact that every exposed rock, river bluff, and railroad embankment was liberally decorated by grafitti in all colors.

I crawled along the interstate out of Massachusetts and into New Hampshire. Finally, I turned off the highway and headed west through the passes of the White Mountains. For the first time rural New England really looked like what I expected from rural New England. There were small towns and villages with neat old homes packed snugly around neat old churches. The White Mountains were a long way short of the Rockies, but they certainly beat out the stumpy Ozarks that hung out around the *Global Query* offices. There had been a snow in the last few days, and the bare limbs of the winter trees bowed under a precariously balanced burden of white. With the vampire dream starting to fade and beautiful rolling hills on all sides, I was actually starting to enjoy myself.

Fifty miles short of my destination, I gave in to growing hunger and pulled off the road to get a bite. There seemed to be a shortage of McDonalds and Burger

Kings in the area, but I did manage to locate a little roadside diner where a waitress in a pink uniform served up a slice of lemon icebox pie big enough that I had to take half of it with me in a box. The choice of meals was not the best thing for my diet, and certainly not the best thing for my diameter-challenged jeans, but I didn't care. After all, if I was going to be alone on this trip, I might as well indulge in my favorite vice.

It was getting dark by the time I dropped a tip on the table and fished the rental car keys from my purse. I was feeling pretty good at this point. A belly full of pie was keeping most thoughts of Jimmy at bay, and the brightly lit, noisy diner was enough to clear the last whispers of the vampire dream from my head. As I opened the door and stepped outside, I was actually whistling.

But the good mood didn't last long. The weather took the first step toward bringing me back to earth. Heavy flakes of snow had begun to fall from the darkening sky—flakes big enough that each of them was almost a preformed snowball. I shivered and pulled my coat tightly closed, but the damp snow splashed against my hair, spattered my face, and hung in my eyelashes. The window of the cars around me were polka-dotted by the snow blobs. I crunched across the gravel parking lot as quickly as I could.

I put the key in the car door and was about to get inside when I spotted the sheet of paper folded under the wiper blade. At first I was only annoyed. I expected it to be an ad for a local church or, considering the size of the servings in the diner, a promotional flyer from some health club. The note was almost hidden by the quickly spreading blanket of snow and when I pulled it free the paper was damp, but the block letters printed on the sheet were still clear.

MEETING MUST BE TONIGHT. 9 PM. Y

That was the extent of the missive—a single line. But the mere fact of the note's presence on my rental car was enough to fill an encyclopedia with implications. My heart literally skipped a beat as I looked at the single-letter signature.

Yorga knew where I was. And if he knew where I was, he had to know when I had landed, he had to know where I rented a car, and he had to know the route I was taking to the inn. In short, he had to be following me.

More than that, this whole interview could be nothing more than a sham to get me out of the office. I was going to Williams Crossing to get some words on paper. But Yorga might not really have any interest in having his story told. His interest might be in telling me things of a more personal nature, or making me the next Bride of the Monster, or in applying nasty pointy things to my skin.

Suddenly my good spirits were replaced by fear at least ten degrees colder than the night air. I raised my head and looked through the white curtains of falling snow. There were a good twenty cars in the diner parking lot, but none of them looked familiar. Of course, until that moment I hadn't been looking for any other vehicle. A whole fleet of Dandy Dan ice-cream trucks could have been playing a constant stream of "Turkey in the Straw" behind me all the way from Boston and I wouldn't have noticed.

I stood there in the cold parking lot with the car door

open and the key alarm chiming at me and wondered what to do next. Moments before, it had seemed that there had been people moving up and down the stairs from the parking lot. There had been noise spilling out through the open door. Now there was not a soul in sight and no sound but the wind whistling around the black pine trees that lined the highway. The woods suddenly seemed very dark. The road heading west to Chester was absolutely devoid of traffic and snow was already beginning to creep onto the gray asphalt like ice forming at the edge of a pond.

One part of me wanted to turn the car back toward Boston. I could get a room for the night somewhere in New Hampshire—somewhere very close to a police station—and be on a flight back to St. Louis first thing in the morning. This line of reasoning was proposed by the rational mind hard at work trying to keep the rest of me out of trouble. But at the end of that very rational journey would come a meeting with my very unrational editor.

Even in my imagination, it was hard to find a good spin for that meeting. Mr. Genovese might not hand me my head for retreating from this interview, but it could well spell the end of my traveling days. I had fought hard to get a chance to investigate stories in person—actual reporting was as rare at the *Query* as a believable story. Unless I wanted to spend the rest of my days at the *Query* doing my field reporting from a cubicle, I had better carry on.

There was also Jimmy to consider. Jimmy had confronted armed guerrillas in Afghanistan and military incompetence in Vietnam. He had risked his life almost daily to bring back his assignments. What would he think of my wimping out on an interview just because someone sent a nonthreatening note? Of course, I didn't really care what Jimmy thought. I didn't need his approval. He was nothing to me. Didn't care at all. Really.

I was still repeating this mental litany when I squeezed into the car, started the engine, and turned the nose toward Vermont.

Just as I pulled out of the parking lot, the door of the diner opened and a bulky figure stepped out onto the top of the stairs. I slowed the car and studied the form in the rearview mirror. It was too far and too dark to see more than an outline, but in this case an outline was enough—from his rotund head to his even more rotund body, I was sure it was the fat man from the plane. No matter how besotted he had become of me during our flight, I doubted any man would follow me across three states on the off chance that I would agree to a cup of coffee. He had to be following me for other reasons. And that meant that the fat man had to be Yorga.

On the one hand, I found this revelation a little reassuring. The guy had seemed pretty harmless back on the plane, and if it came to a confrontation I was pretty sure this was one man I could best in a hundred-yard dash for help. On the other hand, I was more than a little disappointed in my own powers of observation. It was one thing not to spot a car following you along busy highways, but missing a guy the size of Shamu in a small diner took heavy-duty self-involvement.

I pressed the gas and left my portly pursuer behind. If he wanted to have a meeting tonight, he was going to have to catch me.

The snow was falling thick as I rolled down into the valley of the Connecticut River and passed over the long bridge into Vermont. The flakes seemed to come from a single point ahead of me, fanning out around the car to become a tunnel of white. I dug my fingers into the padded steering wheel and drove on resolutely over the bridge and back into hilly terrain as I closed on Williams Crossing and the Stone River Inn.

Apparently there were only a few people with miles to go before they slept on this particular snowy evening, because traffic was very light. I went at least the next ten miles without seeing another vehicle. The snow ahead of me was unmarked by tire tracks. The white blanket lay so prettily across the narrow highway that I almost hated to spoil it.

Then, just as I passed a sign signaling thirty miles between me and my destination, I noticed a glow of light in the rearview mirror. The light brightened quickly. In a few moments, the glow had become the snow-wreathed glare of headlights. Someone was coming down the road behind me in a big, big hurry. In only a matter of seconds, the approaching vehicle had narrowed the gap to a few car lengths.

I moved right until the tires of the rental car were hugging the snowy shoulder of the road in hopes that the vehicle would pass. The other driver had different plans. The lights swung to stay on my tail. And they were still closing. Fast.

I raised my foot, aimed at the brakes, then changed my mind and went for the gas instead. The rental car fishtailed to the side as the tires pawed at the snow-covered road. My heart rose into my throat as the lights grew closer at a furious pace. Gradually, my car began to pick up speed, but it wasn't going to be enough. The lights were fifty feet away. Twenty.

My fingers were holding the wheel so hard, there would probably be a permanent set of prints. I was a half-second away from screaming; only there wasn't a half second left. The lights were twenty feet away. Ten. Zero.

Then the lights were gone.

For a fraction of a second that seemed to stretch into minutes, I sat frozen in my seat, staring out at the darkness through the riot of afterimages stamped into my eyes by the light. Surely I was going to be hit. Maybe I had already been hit. Maybe the impact had smashed the headlights of the oncoming vehicle and my body had just not registered the crunch of metal on metal. Maybe I was milliseconds away from finding out just how hard an air bag could punch me in the chin.

But the milliseconds went by, and several full-sized seconds followed, and no crash came.

I moved my foot to the brake and slowed the car to a stop. My breath echoed in the car like the final exam in a Lamaze class. My heart was beating somewhere just south of my tonsils. Trembling, I opened the door and stepped onto the snowy road.

The road was empty. The only sound was the rumble of the idling car and the constant hiss of the snowflakes striking trees and roadway. There was absolutely no sign of any other car on the road.

But there was something. For just a moment, I was sure I saw a faint glow rising into the dark, cloudy sky, and an even fainter form outlined by the light. Then it was gone.

I stood there with my face to the sky and snowflakes catching in my eyelashes. Working at the *Global Query* had given me plenty of chances to write about UFOs, but this was the first time I had ever seen one.

"I don't even want to believe," I whispered to the night sky. Then I climbed back into my rental car and drove on.

WITH A TIGHTLY WOUND BUN OF GRAY HAIR CLAMPED to the back of her head and a pair of gold-rimmed glasses perched high on her nose, the woman behind the counter could have served as a Norman Rockwell model for Official American Grandma. But the look she gave me as I came in through the double doors of the Stone River Inn was not a "Hi, honey. Come on in out of the cold" kind of look. This was more the "What in the hell did you step in and don't bring any of it in here" sort of look.

I carefully brushed the snow from my boots and ventured a tentative smile. "I'm Savannah McKinnon. I'm supposed to have a room for the—"

"I know who you are," the woman interjected in a stiff tone that was terminated by a sharp sniff. "You're that reporter from the trashy supermarket rag."

Trashy and rag were good descriptions of the *Global Query*, but few people managed to squeeze them into one sentence. If this was an example of New England hospitality, it was easy to see why no one ever bragged about it.

My first thought was to turn around and leave right then. My second thought was that there were a lot of snowy miles between me and the next available warm bed. "That's right, I'm a reporter," I said through my frozen smile. "Do I still get a room? I do have a reservation."

The woman continued to stare for a moment longer. "Well," she said at last, "don't suppose there'll be anyone else along in weather like this and I'm sure I'm not going to get anyone else to stay in *that* room. I might as well give it to you." She picked up a leather-bound book and shoved it across the top of the counter toward me. "Sign this."

Still feeling a little punch-drunk from my strange encounter on a snowy road, I crossed to the table and picked up an imitation quill pen with a ballpoint. "Is something wrong?" I asked as I scribbled my name and address. "I told the person on the phone who I worked for when I reserved the room."

She grabbed the edge of the book and pulled it away. "You didn't tell anybody you were going to be using our rooms to . . . to . . ." Her wrinkles went a level deeper. "To have *relations* with freaks."

Now I was really confused. "Relations? Freaks?"

Before the woman could answer, there was the sound of a bell from another room. "Wait here," said the innkeeper. She hurried around the side of the desk and passed through a set of French doors.

"Can I have the key to my room?" I called after her. There was no reply.

I gave an exhausted sigh and leaned against the

counter. If my hostess left something to be desired, at least the building itself was lovely. The entry of the Stone River Inn was like a temple to smooth wood and simple yankee craftsmanship. The floor was made from thin strips of honey-colored oak that gleamed with fresh wax. The furniture was spare, simple, and probably old enough to have seated Ethan Allen before his name got stuck on overpriced lounge chairs.

There were dark-green braided rugs scattered strategically on the floor, small shelves sprinkled with artifacts of brass and copper, and a massive grandfather clock that rose within inches of the ceiling. The whole place would have been right at home in a magazine photo spread.

I leaned over the register book and flipped through the stiff pages. The Stone River Inn might be pretty, but it didn't do a very good business. The dates between the pages were spread out, with names often a week or two apart. There was one couple that seemed to be regular visitors, but most of the Stone River had to be empty much of the time. The innkeeper should have been glad to get my business, not complaining about it.

"What are you doing?" came a voice from across the room.

I looked up quickly and saw the gray-haired woman striding toward me. "Just waiting. Is my room ready?"

My tone was as pleasant as possible, but the results were anything but. The woman looked from me, wrinkled her nose, and flipped the register book forcefully back to the current page. "Your room is ready and your . . . friend . . . is already there. Now if you—"

"Wait a second." I shook my head vigorously. "What are you talking about? What friend?"

The woman frowned. I had only thought the woman was frowning before. This was frowning. Her mouth puckered so badly that I was afraid she might swallow the upper plate of her dentures. "I don't know what you call it these days," she said, "but he told me he was here to share your room. He knew all about you, so I let him up."

I started to tell her I didn't know what she was talking about, but then I remembered the time on the ornate face of the grandfather clock. The snowy trip over the mountains had put a considerable dent in my schedule. Though I had departed St. Louis in dawn's early daze, it was now only a few minutes before nine. The mysterious—and apparently distasteful—stranger in room six had to be none other than Count Yorga. Somehow, fat boy had gotten a jump on me.

"He's not a friend," I informed the innkeeper. "Just a business associate."

"I see." The innkeeper's glare grew one degree less baleful. "In the future I'd appreciate you doing any business with that man someplace else."

I was still puzzled by her attitude, but I was too busy shoving down my own double dose of disgust to argue. Yorga had not only tracked my car from Boston, now he was actually in my room. For a moment I gave serious consideration to picking up my bags and marching out the door. The quaint village of Williams Crossing was obviously something of a tourist attraction. There had to be someone else with a room available—someone with a room that wasn't already occupied. But once again an innate sense of stubbornness made me stick it out.

I'm sure that it says something about a person's psyche when you're more afraid of embarrassment than of strange men in your hotel room. Probably it says that common sense is not your forte. I preferred to think of it as being a determined journalist.

I bit my lip and looked up the smooth curve of the staircase into the hallway beyond. From where I stood, it was just possible to see a series of dark wooden doors. Behind one of them waited my vampire.

I looked down at the woman behind the desk. "And what was your name?"

The innkeeper's anger was momentarily replaced by confusion. "Mayleen Grimes."

"Nice to meet you Mrs. Grimes." I stuck out my hand and shook hers before the confusion could wear off. "I need you to do me a favor."

Wariness returned quickly to Mrs. Grimes's watery eyes. "What kind of favor?" she asked, pulling her hand free from mine.

I leaned against the counter and lowered my voice to a conspiratorial whisper. "That man upstairs is not supposed to be here."

"He's not?"

"Nope." I glanced over my shoulders at the stairs. "I've never met him before. It's possible he's dangerous."

Mrs. Grimes nodded in agreement. "He looked dangerous." She dropped her own voice to a whisper. "Should I call the police?"

The question was serious enough, but I had to fight to keep myself from smiling. All it took was a taste of danger, and Mayleen Grimes was a different person. The bitter, tight lines of her face were animated by interest and her hands held firmly to the side of the counter. An unpleasant guest was one thing, but a mystery man was something else.

"Let's not involve the police just yet," I said, still whispering. "First I'm going to go up there and see what he wants."

"Should you?" asked the innkeeper. "What if he attacks you? Tries to . . . do things to you."

I gave her a confident smile. "That's where the favor comes in," I said. "I need you to stay right here by the phone. If you hear me yell for help, or if I don't come out in twenty minutes—"

"I should call the sheriff," finished Mrs. Grimes.

"Exactly," I said. "Would you do that for me?"

She nodded eagerly. "Of course, dear. But are you sure you should be doing this?"

"I'll be fine." I flashed another confident I'm-a-seasoned-professional, don't-try-this-at-home grin and turned for the stairs. "Twenty minutes," I called over my shoulder. "Start timing me."

I felt pretty good as I started up the steps. I had turned an enemy into an ally. I had stuck to my guns and faced my fears. But with each step I took toward the room in question, I felt those fears growing. After all, everything I had told Mrs. Grimes was more or less true. Yorga was an unknown quantity. Even if he was a butterball, he might really be dangerous. I hoped the innkeeper kept her ears peeled for a scream.

I reached into my purse, fumbled past a hodgepodge of supplies, and wrapped my fingers around a spray bottle of pepper mace. There was a difference between determination and stupidity. If the count turned out to be a loonie who had a yen to plant dime-store fangs in my throat, he was going to discover the joys of a face full of capsicum.

Fortified against pseudo-immortal badies, I turned toward room six and knocked lightly against the dark wood panel. "Hello," I called through the door. "Is anyone there?"

There was an immediate rustling sound from the other side of the door. "You're late," said an accented voice I recognized from the telephone.

I almost laughed. "Late for what? You're not even supposed to be here."

"The note said nine o'clock."

"It's nine o'clock now," I replied.

"Five after," said Yorga. "The clock downstairs is slow." There was a metallic tap, then a snap. The door opened less than an inch. "Hurry up," the voice hissed through the narrow opening. "Get in here and do your interview before I change my mind."

The pettiness of Yorga's tone irritated me, but in a way it also reassured me. Somehow, anyone that bickered over a couple of minutes didn't seem like a candidate for serial killer. Just in case, I kept one hand wrapped around the bottle of pepper spray. With the other I pressed open the door.

Light from the hallway spilled over the light, glossy boards of an oak floor. Beyond this shining trapezoid, the room was filled with an impenetrable darkness. I edged forward and squinted into the gloom. "Um, maybe we should meet somewhere else," I suggested.

"No," Yorga snapped from the shadows. "Here or nowhere. If you want your interview, come in here and get it."

I swallowed. Suddenly, an image from my dream on

the plane reappeared in my mind. Bone-white flesh. Curving fangs. As silly as it seemed, the flashback brought a bitter taste deep in my throat.

No sooner was I through the door than I felt something rush past. I caught only a blur of movement before the door slammed shut, plunging the room into total darkness. It was all I could do to stifle a scream.

"Now," Yorga said from somewhere very close by, "let's get down to business."

"Lights," I replied. My voice was so choked it was little more than a squeak.

"What?" asked the count.

I cleared my throat. "Can we at least turn on a light? I need to see if I'm going to take notes."

For a few seconds, the was no sound in the darkened room. Then I heard soft footfalls and rustling cloth as Yorga moved away.

"All right," he said. "I'll turn on one light, understand? Only one. More would be dangerous."

The darkness was already starting to seem as heavy as a blanket. I nodded, then remembered that no one could see me. "Yeah, any light would be good."

With a sharp click, a hooded desk lamp snapped to life. The cone of light it cast was dim, spreading weakly cover a small round table and a pair of high-backed chairs. The reflected glow was just enough to get my first good look at the vampire.

My reaction was perfectly professional. "Holy shit!" I screamed.

FIVE

RESEARCHERS ATTEMPTING TO FIND A CURE FOR THE common cold had missed one big factor—the healing properties of fear. One moment of sheer terror did a better job of clearing my head than a drugstore full of decongestants. Apparently, nature has ordained that dying in horror is enough, no one should deal with both death and a runny nose.

I backed up against the door so hard that the wood creaked on its frame. The pepper spray dropped from my numb fingers. *Scream,* said a strident voice in my skull. *Scream loud. Scream long. This is not a drill.*

But screaming was out of the question. My head might be clear, but my already overly snug jeans suddenly seemed way, way too tight—too tight to allow breathing, much less screaming. I could only stand frozen by the door while little red sparks swam across my vision and my knees threatened to turn to guava jelly.

''Would you like me to turn off the lamp?'' asked the man at the center of the room.

That woke me up. "No," I said in a forced whisper. The only thing more frightening than the idea of being in the room with this man was being in a dark room with this man.

"As you wish." The man stepped back slightly from the lamp, allowing shadows to fall across his face. It helped. A little. "Are you ready to begin?" he asked. "Time is short."

I fumbled behind me until one of my hands fell on the comforting round flank of the doorknob. With that bit of metal in hand, I found my breath coming a little easier. "What's wrong with you?" I choked out. It was not the most politically correct question I had ever asked, but it certainly was sincere.

In the none-too-bright glow of the desk lamp, the vampire's face was every bit as strange as that of my nightmare. Yorga had absolutely no resemblance to the fat man I had seen on the plane and again at the diner. In fact, he was so thin you could have cut yourself on the angles of his face. His skin might not have been quite as white as the saber-toothed vampire of airline dreamland, but it was close—a chalky, dead color that reminded me of mushrooms, grubs, and fish bellies. Worse, where his skin wasn't a dull white, it was streaked by twisting blue veins and broken webs of red capillaries. Scars ridged his forehead and there were blisters along his cheeks. The circles that ringed his eyes were so dark, it almost looked like they were floating in tar pits. Bruises covered the skin around his mouth and along his neck. The mass of hair on his head was white as cobwebs and just about as limp.

I shivered. Somewhere in the back of my mind—and often in the front—I had pictured myself as a tireless, fearless journalist. I indulged myself with visions of following troops into battle, ducking mortar fire in some beleaguered city, and confronting politicians with their real voting records. Trembling with fear had not been part of the picture. But then, neither had facing down vampires.

The count was slow to respond to my question. While I continued to cling to the doorknob, he sat down in one of the high-backed chairs and surrendered himself to a fit of coughing. To the great relief of my remaining shreds of sanity, the coughs revealed no curving four-inch fangs, but Yorga's mouth was still not a pretty sight. Yellowed teeth jutted from gums that were a deep purple. Just the play of the light over his raw, pasty flesh was enough to raise a fresh crop of goose bumps along my arms.

"Are you surprised at my appearance, Ms. McKinnon?" he asked once the storm had passed.

I started to shake my head, froze a moment in indecision, then managed a nod. "Yeah."

"And how did you expect a vampire to look?"

"I didn't . . . I don't . . ." I stammered to a halt, fought for a breath, and tried again. "I didn't think you were—"

"Actually a vampire?" Yorga sneered. "You were perfectly willing to write it in your paper, but you didn't believe."

He had me there. But if I only wrote stories for the *Query* that I actually believed, most of my pieces would end at my byline. I swallowed a bit of my fear and stepped away from the door. "I'm still not sure I believe you're a vampire." That was being diplomatic. There were no such things as vampires. I was at least 76 percent sure of this fact.

Yorga shook his head. "It doesn't matter what you think," he said. "If you report my words accurately, you can believe anything you like."

Now that my heart was no longer throttling my brain, another fact came bouncing between my ears. "My name," I said. "You know my name."

"Of course."

"Not my pen name," I went on. "You said, 'Ms. McKinnon,' not Ms. Skye."

Yorga's face might have been horrible, but it was expressive enough to show disgust at my question. "Some of us actually do a little research," he said.

That barb was all it took to change a fragment of my fear into anger. "Right, and I suppose some of this research involved following me?"

The count waved a gloved hand through the air. "Contacting you was necessary," he maintained stiffly. "Time for our meeting was running out."

"Why was that?" I asked.

Yorga glanced around at the windows on the far side of the room and spoke in a low voice. "A vampire has many enemies."

In my opinion, anyone that followed people, snuck into hotel rooms, and generally behaved like a jerk was very likely to pick up enemies—vampire or not. "What about that little trick on the highway?" I asked. "I suppose that was all part of the game?"

The vampire pursed his bloodless lips. "What trick?"

"Running me off the road back there," I said, jerking my thumb in the general direction of New Hampshire.

"I don't have any idea what you're talking about,"

said Yorga, "but if you drive no better than you write, it's a wonder you ever find the road in the first place."

Now it was my turn to growl. I reached into my purse and fumbled past the pepper spray to find my notepad and pen. "All right," I said. "Let's get this over so I can go home and you can go back to the cemetery."

"Perfect," said Yorga. He settled in his chair and rested his gloved hands on the knees of his dark pants. "Just be sure you record my words accurately."

"Oh, right," I replied. "It would be terrible if something like a name or date got messed up." I stepped forward cautiously, snagged the back of the nearest chair, and pulled it a few feet closer to the door. Then I stepped around and dropped into the seat. This far from the lamp it was something of a challenge to see my pad, but at least I was out of reach should Yorga decide to stop talking and start feeding.

I squinted down at the list of questions I had written on the plane. "How did you become a vampire?"

Yorga was silent for a moment. I expected him to make some comment on the lameness of the question. Instead, he reached inside his rough black jacket and pulled out a sheaf of papers. "I was born north of a village called Orange in the year 1428," he said with all the conviction of a man reading a legal brief.

The date didn't jibe with the age the count had argued about so vigorously only the day before, but I wrote it down dutifully. All I wanted was to get this over with and get away. Yorga might be a fake vampire, but he was a genuine creep.

"Some thirty years later, a man named Shoreham came to our village," the count continued. "It was in that same year that I—" he broke off abruptly and turned around in his chair. ''Did you hear that?'' he whispered.

I paused in my scribbling. ''What?''

''Shhhh,'' hissed Yorga. ''Quiet, you idiot.'' He quickly pushed back his chair, dropped to his hands and knees, and began to crawl across the floor.

I looked at him in shock. It was one thing to interview a man who thought he was a vampire, another to share a room with one of the hounds of Dracula. ''What are you doing?''

Yorga scrambled around the foot of the bed and crawled up below the row of windows. ''There's some-one out there,'' he whispered.

''Out where?''

''Outside, you fool.'' He raised his head slightly and peered over the lip of the windowsill.

I squinted across the room toward the bank of win-dows. The window was as old-fashioned as the rest of the Stone River Inn. Strips of white-painted wood di-vided glass that had the slightly uneven look of genuine age. Little light leaked in through the small, thick panes and what there was showed nothing but the branches of trees layered with snow. ''You know, this *is* the second floor,'' I said. ''How can anyone be outside?''

''Be quiet, idiot,'' Yorga replied without looking at me. He began to cough, but he smothered the sound. Even in the dim light I could see his back shaking with the effort of suppressing the coughs.

Between his psychotic actions and his illness, I almost felt sorry for him. ''What's wrong?'' I asked. ''Do you think there's another vampire flying around out there?''

The count turned to face me. His eyes reflected the lamplight with an eerie reddish glow and there was a sneer on his pale, mottled face. ''You really are both ignorant and stupid,'' he said in a harsh whisper. ''You deserve to work for a worthless rag like the *Global Query*.''

Okay, so I didn't feel sorry for him any more. ''Fine.'' I snapped my notebook shut. ''You keep looking for bats. This interview is over.''

''No!'' The count forgot both his whispering and his accent as he whirled around. He stood up and waved his fistful of notes through the air. ''You must record my statement.''

''I don't have to do anything,'' I replied. I shoved the notebook back into my purse and stood up. ''You want to go talk to the *Weekly World News*? You go right ahead.''

Yorga's face was capable of at least one more emotion—fear. His red-tinted eyes went wide and his mouth tightened in a grimace. ''This interview must go on. It could be my last chance.''

The quaver in his voice was enough to make me delay my exit. I glanced past him at the dark glass of the window. ''What's out there?'' I asked. ''What are you afraid of?''

A milk-pale tongue slipped from his mouth and licked at his lips. He turned his back on me and paced across the room. ''You wouldn't understand.''

I nodded. ''Because I'm just a dumb tabloid journalist?''

''No!'' He shook his head again. His white hair flew around his forehead like cotton. ''No, that's not what I meant.''

The change in his demeanor was amazing. One minute he had looked on me as a lower form of life, but the threat of ending the interview had catapulted me up the evolutionary ladder. I took my notebook back out and opened the cover. ''Then what are you afraid of?'' I asked. ''Von Helsing? Buffy?''

Yorga started to answer, then he whirled toward the window. This time I heard the sound that had attracted his attention. It was a clicking sound—somewhere between a branch scratching against a house and someone flicking a fingernail against a drinking glass. It sounded twice in close succession, paused, then three more times. Click. Click. Click.

I took a step toward the window. ''What is that?''

''Nuuhh,'' said Yorga.

''What?''

The count took a slow step, started to turn, and fell to his knees.

''Yorga?'' I moved toward him, but stayed out of reach. Vampires are known to be tricky.

''Uhhhh,'' the count moaned. The vampire fell forward on his face so quickly that I could hear the crunch as his nose broke his fall.

''Yorga!''

Casting caution aside, I hurried up to the fallen man and tried to turn him over. He was heavy and his body jerked with erratic tremors, but I managed to raise his face from the floor. What I saw almost made me let go.

Blood flowed from Yorga's smashed nose, but it was very curious blood. Even in the dim light it seemed far too pale—pale and translucent with a color that was more violet than red. There was a equally pale purple foam dripping from his open mouth.

My own legs felt weak and my stomach did a flip-flop. I didn't know whether to help him up, dial nine-one-one, or pull out a cross. "Count Yorga?" I said in a voice that trembled too much for my liking. "Can you hear me?"

The vampire's eyes fluttered open. "I . . . I . . ." he mumbled.

I leaned in closer. "Yes?"

And that was when he bit me. His back arced. His boot heels drummed the floor. His teeth clamped down on my forearm.

For a moment I could only stare in shock. Then the nerves in my skin woke up and reminded me that teeth penetrating my epidermis tended to hurt. Lots. I twisted, pulled, and finally tore my bleeding forearm away from his mouth. The heels of my shoes scrapped at the oaken boards as I scrambled back across the floor. "What are you doing?" I cried.

Yorga raised his head. Mixed with the purple foam on his chin were streaks of dark-red blood—my blood. "Run . . . from . . ." However he intended to finish this sentence, he was interrupted by a flood of violet fluid that boiled up and over his stained teeth.

With one last spasm and a passable death rattle, the vampire collapsed on the floor.

Now? asked the little voice in my head.

Oh, yes. Definitely.

I opened my mouth and screamed.

SIX

YOU CAN TELL A LOT ABOUT A TOWN BY THE LOOKS OF its police station. In some cities the station is built like a fortress to guard against fear—lots of guns, metal desks, and concrete. In rich towns stations can be palaces dedicated to the gods of high-tech security, filled with enough gadgets to stock a Batcave.

In Williams Crossing the police station was more like a janitor's office. The whole thing was contained in a single narrow room at the back of an old brick building: two desks, four chairs, and a lonely shotgun locked in an otherwise empty wall rack. So far as I could see, there were no fax machines, no computers, and nothing that could pass for a jail cell. Either there was not much crime in Williams Crossing that called for being locked up, or they made it a practice to shoot offenders on the spot.

I sat in a hard red-plastic chair across from one of the desks and rubbed my wounded arm. A local doctor had cleaned and dressed the set of teeth marks in my forearm, but I swore the wound was still crawling with nasty vampire germs. Any minute I expected to grow fangs and a pair of leathery bat wings.

From the way the other occupant of the station kept staring at me, you would have thought the wings were already sprouting.

With his ginger hair and a mustache so thin it gave peach fuzz a bad name, Sheriff's Deputy Douglas Yeager looked young enough to be a fan of Barney tapes. Behind his battered green metal desk, he wore dark-blue pants with crisply ironed seams, a pale-blue shirt that had come untucked in the back, and an expression that was frozen somewhere between wonderment and terror.

"Could you see him in the window?" asked the deputy.

I puzzled over this for a moment, then shook my head. "I don't understand. See who?"

He glanced frequently between me and the darkened windows at the front of the small room. If there had been a garland of garlic handy, I was sure he would have been wearing it. "The vampire. You said he walked over by the window."

"Yeah." I nodded.

"So? Could you see him in the glass?"

It took me a moment more, but I finally figured out what the deputy was after. "Do you want to know if I could see his reflection?"

Deputy Doug nodded eagerly. "Did you?"

I shrugged. "I don't remember."

This answer was obviously a great disappointment. The deputy thought for a moment, then ventured another deft probe. "Did you feel anything when he bit you?"

"Feel anything?" I leaned forward in my chair and spoke in a fearful whisper. "You mean like a dark essence entering my soul and dragging me into a lightless world of eternal damnation?''

The deputy's blue eyes went wide. ''Yeah.''

I shook my head. ''All I felt was teeth.''

The deputy pushed his lips out in a pout and looked away. ''Fine,'' he said. ''If you don't want to talk about it, that's fine.''

Silence was certainly fine with me. For the last three hours, I had done little but answer the same questions over and over. An ambulance had shown up at the Stone River Inn in response to my frantic calls for help, and Mrs. Grimes's button-pushing. The med techs had been on the scene within twenty minutes, but by then there was no doubt that Count Yorga's bid for true immortality was over.

Since then, there had been a whirlwind of activity—or at least what passed for a whirlwind in Williams Crossing. Yorga's body had gone off to the coroner. I had gone to the doctor for three stitches, a bandage, and disinfectant. Then it was twenty questions time with the sheriff. So far, they hadn't quite gotten around to accusing me of killing the count, but there was no doubt I was considered a potential vampire slayer.

A bell jingled over the front door as the sheriff came back into the office. Coming in was a good thirty-second process for the sheriff. Where Deputy Doug looked like a candidate for sixth grade, Sheriff Bob Loudermilk looked like a candidate for being six feet under.

The sheriff wore the same navy slacks and cornflower shirt as his deputy—actual badges appeared to be too ostentatious for Williams Crossing—but on the sheriff the clothing hung as loose as bedsheets. Loudermilk's face was clamped in tight against his skull and his scalp had more liver spots than hair. His movements were so slow it looked as if someone was running a film at the wrong speed. If Yorga had been telling the truth about being four hundred years old, he and the sheriff might have been childhood friends.

Deputy Doug popped to attention as the sheriff came in. "Everything's fine here, Sheriff."

Loudermilk looked at him with cool gray eyes. "And is there any reason it shouldn't be fine?"

"No, Sheriff."

"Good." The sheriff finished his slow entry and pulled the door closed behind him. "I didn't leave you with any chores but to watch this young lady. I would hope you can manage the task without stirring too much trouble."

I cleared my throat. "Speaking of watching me," I interjected, "do you think there's a chance I could leave now?"

Loudermilk made a noncommittal grunt. He walked slowly across the room to the open desk and eased himself into a padded chair. "The coroner's already had a look at your dead boy. Seems there's no obvious signs of injury." He rubbed at the gray stubble on his chin with a knob-knuckled hand. "Looks like this Yorga fella was sick six ways from Sunday. Coroner says he might have died from natural causes. Heart failure, most likely."

The odds of Yorga dropping dead of a heart attack right at that moment seemed about as likely as my odds of taking over CNN, but I wasn't about to voice any objections. I stood up and stretched the cramps out of my legs. "Good," I said. "If it was natural causes, then I guess I can leave."

"You might think so," said the sheriff, "but it seems like we'll be needing you a bit longer."

Exhaustion tugged at my eyelids. "Can't you just call me in the morning?" I begged.

Loudermilk shook his bald head. "There's a state man on the way from Montpelier. Should be here any minute."

I groaned. The prospect of repeating my tale a few dozen more times was not appealing. "I already told you everything. Can't you talk to the state troopers for me?"

"It's not the troopers who want you," said the sheriff. "This fellow's from the state bureau of investigation."

That information was enough to scrape off the first layer of my drowsiness. "Does the state investigate all deaths you report?"

Loudermilk gave a humorless snort. "Never came to investigate anything I reported." He pulled open a desk drawer, extracted a fistful of forms, and plopped them down on the scratched wooden surface. "But I didn't call them in on this one. They called me."

Sleep took another step down the pyramid of immediate needs. "If you didn't call them, then how did they find out about the murder?" I asked.

"Nobody said this was a murder," said the sheriff. "Far as how the state boys found out . . ." He shrugged. "I don't know, and the truth is, I don't care."

From the corner of my eye I saw Deputy Doug grinning. Apparently the deputy enjoyed seeing me hit a stone wall when it came to extracting information from the sheriff. I gritted my teeth and went in for another try.

"What would make the state bureau of investigation interested in Count Yorga?" I asked.

Sheriff Loudermilk licked the pointed end of a pencil and began to make careful entries on his forms. "Don't know that either," he replied without looking up.

Deputy Doug laughed. "Looks like you're not going to get any stories for your drugstore paper here."

The sheriff looked over at his assistant. "Douglas?"

"Yes, Sheriff?"

"Shut up."

The deputy looked down. "Yes, Sheriff."

Before I could think of anything more to ask, the door to the sheriff's office opened with such force that the little bell was sent flying across the room. A barrel-chested man squeezed into the already-cramped space and slammed the door behind him. The newcomer was middle-aged, with a rumpled tan trench coat that gapped open to reveal an even more rumpled suit. There was a good mix of gray in his russet hair, a shadow of dark beard along his cheeks, and enough stains on his clothes to provide a good menu of his meals for the last week. There was an air about him of someone who had been there, seen that, and cleaned it all off the bottom of his shoe.

He stomped into the tiny room and scanned across it quickly until his dark eyes fixed on me. "You must be Savvy McKinnon," he said in a firm dry voice.

It wasn't exactly a great piece of detective work considering that I was the only woman in the room, and the person delivering this line was not the cleanest character I had ever met; but after a few hours with Loudermilk and company, I was relieved to hear someone that sounded like he knew which end was up. I had high hopes that I was ten seconds from being sent off in search of precious sleep.

"That's right," I replied.

Wrinkled suit nodded. "Good." He stepped back and jerked open the door he had just closed. "Come with me."

These weren't quite the comforting words I had expected. I shivered under the freezing gusts from outside and studied the man's blunt features. "Before we go anywhere, would you mind telling me who you are?"

The question seemed to cause the newcomer a great deal of annoyance. The door slammed a second time, cutting off the cold wind from outside. He rolled his eyes and heaved a sigh before reaching into his coat to produce a dark leather badge holder. "Special Agent Frank Hoskins, FBI."

I opened my mouth in surprise. Hoskins was not quite what I expected in an FBI agent.

"What's the FBI doing here?" Sheriff Loudermilk asked. "We never asked for you boys. We were expecting someone from Montpelier."

Agent Hoskins flipped the badge case closed and shoved it back inside his jacket. "The state authorities won't be making an appearance. I've contacted them and let them know that the FBI will be taking over this case."

The sheriff's thin lips tightened. "Why would the FBI be interested in some sick fella dying of a heart attack?"

Loudermilk was doing such a good job asking questions that I wished I had my tape recorder ready. Agent Hoskins took a second to answer, but when he did the words poured out quickly. "Michael Willmeyer has been one of our most wanted for over two years."

This time I beat the sheriff to the next question. "Who's Michael Wilmer?"

"Willmeyer," Hoskins corrected. He shoved his hands into the pockets of his trench coat. "That would be your dead man."

"He told me his name was Yorga," I said.

The agent rolled his eyes again. "Gee, he lied to you. I guess wanted criminals have a habit of doing that."

I could feel color rushing to my cheeks. "He was a criminal?"

"Bank robber," Hoskins said with a nod. "Now, can we go see your dead vampire before the sun comes up? I'd hate to go back to Langley with nothing but a pile of ash."

FOR A SMALL TOWN, WILLIAMS CROSSING SURE HAD more than its share of dead people.

The local morgue—which actually turned out to be the basement of Armistead and Sons Funeral Parlor—was packed with six long metal tables. Five of these held silent forms neatly tucked beneath pale blue sheets. On the sixth table Count Yorga lay with the sheet pulled down and his white face exposed to all comers.

In death, the vampire count didn't look too different than he had in life—or undeath, or whatever it was that vampires called their existence. His skin was still deathly pale, only now it seemed a little more appropriate to his condition. The splashes of color that marred his white face had faded like old tattoos, leaving him looking something like a man that had been rolled in flour.

Arrayed around the bodies like a band of outnumbered mourners were me, Sheriff Loudermilk, and Agent Hoskins. Despite considerable whining, Deputy Doug had been left behind to guard the fort. Sheriff

Loudermilk had come along to make sure the county's interests were represented. So far as I could tell, he was representing those interests by snoozing in a metal folding chair.

"Is there some reason I have to be here?" I asked. Even if I did want "tough-as-nails crime reporter" tacked onto my resume, spending time around dead people was way down on my list of priorities.

"Efficiency," said Hoskins. "I need to talk to you, I need to take a look at the body." He shrugged. "Might as well do it all in one place."

"Wonderful." I wrinkled my nose at the odor that permeated the room—a thick mixture of formalin, makeup, and things I did not even want to identify. As long as Agent Hoskins's questions didn't take the rest of the night, the stink might still be worth it. The revelation that thc vampire I had interviewed was actually a wanted criminal offered a chance at a decent story. It might be a little too sensible for the *Global Query*, and it wasn't the story I had been sent to collect, but it would do in a pinch.

"How about a few answers from your side," I asked. I reached back into my purse and pulled out my trusty notepad for what seemed like the tenth time in twenty-four hours. "Tell me about this Michael Willmeyer."

"Sorry," Hoskins replied, "the FBI doesn't answer questions. We just ask them." The agent pulled a red-and-white-striped mint from his pocket, dropped the cellophane wrapper to the floor, and popped the candy in his mouth. He moved over beside the table and pulled the sheet back from Yorga's body. I had a glimpse of white shoulders, white chest, white stomach—white things I definitely did not want to see.

I turned away. "Can you at least tell me what Willmeyer is supposed to have done?" After a few moments of silence, I risked a glimpse over my shoulder. "Agent Hoskins?"

"He killed a policeman," the agent mumbled in reply. Hoskins reached into his trench coat and pulled out first a pair of black-rimmed glasses, then a white surgical mask. With jerky motion he shoved the glasses up the bridge of his nose. Then he slipped the mask over his head and settled it on his face.

I stood up, took a step toward him, then took a step back. "I thought you said Willmeyer was a bank robber."

"He killed a policeman while robbing a bank," Hoskins replied quickly, his voice muffled by the mask. He leaned over the body until his face was only inches from Yorga's blotched white skin.

I frowned in distaste. Despite the disgusting sight of Yorga's blotchy form, I couldn't look away. "What are you doing?"

"Looking for evidence." The agent reached into his coat again and came out with a pair of heavy, yellow rubber gloves—gloves that looked more suited to floor-scrubbing than surgery—and began to slide his thick fingers inside.

"What's with all the gear?" I asked.

"Willmeyer was obviously ill," said the agent. "I have to take precautions."

There was a squeak of hinges as the double doors at the end of the room swung open. "What this guy had isn't contagious," said a voice from the hall. "This condition was inherited."

A new figure stepped into the room. He was tall, with

long legs and broad shoulders beneath the jacket of a dark-blue, single-breasted suit. He had neatly combed jet-black hair over a high forehead that sloped down to bright blue eyes, a strong but not-too-large nose, and a square chin. If the rumpled Hoskins was an FBI special agent, this guy had to be some kind of super agent: an American James Bond.

Agent Hoskins paused in putting on his gloves and pressed his glasses up the bridge of his nose with one rubber-coated finger. He sized up the newcomer with an emotionless stare. "Who are you with?" he asked. "I thought I told those guys in Stovington to stay out of this."

"I'm not from Stovington," said the Bond-a-like. "I'm a son."

For the first time, Agent Hoskins's face expressed an actual emotion. "What do you mean, a son?" he asked with obvious confusion.

"A son," the handsome stranger repeated. "As in Armistead and Sons." He jerked his thumb toward the ceiling. "My father owns this place."

Hoskins gave a little snort. "I see." He snapped on his remaining glove and went back to the examination of my former interview subject.

I felt a little disappointed myself. "You're a mortician?"

The dashing stranger turned to me with a bright, ready smile. "Not really. I'm still in school." He offered a well-manicured hand. "Cooper Armistead."

"Savannah McKinnon," I replied, taking his hand. I gave myself something of a mental kick for forgetting to use my pen name. Savvy Skye didn't have all the drawbacks of a real person—like a phone that rang in the middle of the night and an address where she could be waylaid by weirdoes—but once my name was out, it was too late to grab it back.

Cooper smiled. ''A lovely name. How appropriate that it should belong to you.''

Okay, so he was a mortician-in-training. At least he was a charming mortician. I extracted my hand from his. ''What were you saying about an inherited condition?''

Cooper strolled into the room and stood next to Agent Hoskins as the FBI man peered down at Yorga. ''This man suffered from a severe form of porphyria,'' said Armistead.

''Is that so?'' Hoskins barely glanced at the man in the dark suit before returning to his examination of the body. ''What do you know about porphyria?''

''It's a whole range of disorders involving enzymes in the blood,'' said the death-doctor-to-be in a confident tone. ''Technically, they cause accumulation of porphyrins. The effects can be anything from skin rashes to nervous-system damage.'' He picked up one of Yorga's stiff hands and turned it over. ''See these blisters on the back of his hand? That's a typical problem for acute porphyria sufferers who are exposed to sunlight.''

The information was a little dry, but there was at least one point that contained the seeds of a good sidebar on my vampire story. ''So you're saying that this man was allergic to sunlight?'' I asked.

Armistead dropped Yorga's dead hand and turned toward me. ''It's not really an allergy, but in acute cases even a brief exposure to sun can cause blisters, scarring, and possibly more serious problems.''

I overcame my squeamish stomach and took a good look at the dead man. Sure enough, the scars and blotches on his pale skin were limited to his hands, neck, and face—the areas that might have been exposed to sun. "Could he actually have died from too much sun?"

The mortician-in-training shrugged his shoulders. "Porphyria can certainly be fatal. We won't know until the tests come back."

"But I thought the coroner said he died of a heart attack."

Armistead laughed. "My dad's the coroner." He rapped his knuckles against the nearest metal table. "He says everyone without a twelve-guage hole in their head died of a heart attack. His medical knowledge stops at finding the organs so he can take them out. If you want a real autopsy, this guy will have to go down to the state facility."

I thought for a moment of the story possibilities. VAMPIRE DISEASE KILLS COUNT YORGA. KILLER COUNT DEAD FROM SUNSHINE. Given a chance to work on the story, I was sure I could work up something that was nicely catchy and suitably sleazy. It wasn't the interview I had been sent to collect, and it was certainly the last story we were likely to collect from Count Yorga, but at least it was a story.

A smile started to form on my lips. Then it froze. I glanced down at the man on the table and started to feel a little queasy. Not because of the dead man's scars, but because of the way I was acting.

A man was dead. He had dropped dead in the same room with me, practically died in my arms, and all I was thinking about was a story. Maybe it meant I was turning into a seasoned journalist. Maybe it meant I was becoming a heartless bitch.

"Hey, are you all right?"

I blinked and saw Cooper Armistead looking down at me with concern. ''Yeah,'' I said. ''Yeah, I'm fine. Just tired.''

He smiled gently. ''Why don't we get out of here and see if you can find a place to get a cup of coffee?''

Before I could answer, Agent Hoskins stood up and snapped off his rubber gloves. ''We'll be sending a team for the body,'' he said. ''They should be here by dawn.''

''You're taking Yorga—I mean Willmeyer—away?'' I asked.

''As soon as possible,'' Hoskins replied. He removed his mask and glasses and stuffed them back into his coat. ''Now, if I can just ask you a few questions, my work here will be done.''

Armistead made an gallant attempt to intervene. ''Can't this wait?'' he asked. ''It's well after midnight, and Ms. McKinnon is clearly exhausted.''

I glanced at the mortician from the corner of my eye. I had a strong suspicion that the only reason he was interested in getting me in a bed was because he was hoping to share the sheets, but I was anxious to avoid another round of twenty questions. ''I already told the sheriff everything I know,'' I said. ''You can get your information from him.''

The agent took a quick look at the sleeping man in the corner, then shook his head. ''I prefer to get my information from the source.''

I sighed. It seemed I still had miles to go before I slept. ''What do you want to know?''

Now it was Hoskins's turn to produce a notepad and pen. He pulled the supplies from the apparently endless depths of his trench coat, flipped open the cover of the notepad, and looked at me. "Where did you meet Mr. Willmeyer?"

"At the Stone River Inn."

"That's here in Williams Crossing?" he asked.

I nodded.

Hoskins scribbled for a moment. "Do you have any idea why Willmeyer was in your room?" asked the agent.

I nodded. "He was there to meet me."

The FBI agent frowned at this news. "You knew Willmeyer?"

"Sort of." I gave a quick review of my brief history as the biographer of the not-so-great but definitely late Count Yorga. "So we were supposed to meet up here last night and get the definitive chapter in his life as a vampire," I concluded, "but Willmeyer never got a chance to give me the interview."

For a good thirty seconds there was no sound in the room but the soft snoring of Sheriff Loudermilk. Agent Hoskins could not have looked more stunned if I had hit him across the forehead with a tire iron. He stared off into space with his mouth hanging open and a flush slowly growing on his stubbled face.

It was Armistead that broke the silence. "Now can she go?" he asked. "She's told you everything she knows."

Hoskins shook his head slowly. "Right there," he said in a hushed, awe-struck tone. "Right there in front of us. In front of *everybody*."

"What?" I asked.

"Nothing." The FBI agent raised his head and fixed his eyes on me. "Do you know where I can get a copy of this *Global Query*?"

''Yeah,'' I said with a nod. ''Try four hundred thousand supermarkets coast to coast.''

Hoskins still seemed stunned. He looked at me for a moment, then turned slowly to look at the pale body on the cold metal table. ''We'll have to get Willmeyer out of here before morning,'' he said slowly.

''My dad will be glad to hear that,'' said Armistead. ''We're really low on space and all the viewing halls are overbooked.''

The agent didn't even seem to hear the interruption. He turned to stare blankly at me for a few moments longer, then nodded. ''All right, Ms. McKinnon. You can go.''

As soon as he spoke those words I felt as if a heavy blanket of fatigue had dropped over me. I raised a tired hand in a ineffective attempt to hide a yawn. ''That's great,'' I said once I had the yawn out of my system. I looked over to where Loudermilk sat nodding in his chair. ''I guess I need to wake the sheriff if I'm going to get a ride back to the inn.''

''Don't bother,'' Armistead said quickly. He slipped a hand into his suit and came out with a ring of jingling keys. ''I can give you a lift.''

I took a moment to consider my options. Normally, I made it a rule not to accept rides from strange morticians in the middle of the night. But as long as Armistead was willing to make the proposal in front of an FBI agent, I figured his intentions must be at least moderately honorable. ''All right,'' I said. ''Let's go.''

Armistead held open the swinging doors, but Agent Hoskins called before we could slip away.

''Ms. McKinnon?''

I looked back over my shoulder. ''Yes?''

"You weren't thinking of leaving town, were you?" asked the FBI man.

"Well, actually . . ."

"Don't."

I sighed. "Right. I'll stick around." Back when I had thought the interview was going to be followed by a romantic weekend with Jimmy, I had reserved the room at the Stone River Inn for the whole weekend. It looked like I was going to use that reservation whether I liked it or not.

In a half-asleep daze, I followed Armistead up the stairs, down a darkened hallway, and out into the cold parking lot. Under the lights along the edge of the lot, scattered snowflakes were falling in slow ballets from a black sky. At least two inches of fresh snow already lay on the roads. I shivered and pulled my coat tight.

"Where are you staying?" asked Armistead as he led the way onto the slippery asphalt.

"At the Stone River Inn." I paused and tried to force a thought through my exhausted mind. "Or at least I was staying there. I didn't leave my room in the best of conditions." That was putting it mildly. I had left the room with puddles of vampire blood pooling on the floor and a dead body lying on the rug. "The innkeeper might not be exactly overjoyed to see me back."

"No problem," said Armistead without turning. "You can stay with me."

I was just tired enough that his offer seemed more silly than bothersome. A giggle slipped out between my lips and I had to fight to hold down more laughter. "No thanks. The Stone River Inn will be fine."

If my laughing at Armistead caused him any embarrassment, he didn't let it show. Instead he guided me through the nearly empty parking lot to a charcoal Mercedes SUV.

"Dying must be popular," I said as I climbed into the soft butter-cream pale leather seats.

The young mortician grinned. "Dying is always popular," he said. "My family has been funeral parlor barons ever since the 1919 flu killed half the county and left us with most of the money." He cranked the big vehicle and began steering it onto the snow-packed road. "We used to have three more parlors in other towns, but my dad sold out to a national chain." He glanced at me and smiled. "It was an offer we couldn't refuse."

I leaned back against the cozy leather upholstery and let my eyes slide shut. "I guess you're never short of customers," I said. Then I felt that exhausted giddiness come over me again. "As long as you don't have a town full of vampires."

"So this guy really did tell you he was a vampire?" Armistead asked.

"Yeah." I nodded without opening my eyes.

For a few minutes there was only the soft sound of the big Mercedes cutting through the snow. Then the mortician spoke again. "Funny that he should call himself Yorga."

I opened one eye. "Why is that funny?"

"It's from a movie," he said. "Several movies, actually."

I managed to push sleep back far enough to realize this was information I should know. "What movies? I never heard the name before."

Armistead laughed. "I'd be surprised if you had." He steered around a corner and stole a glance in my direction. "Count Yorga was the main character in a B-movie vampire series from American Internation. An actor named Robert Quarry played this vampire count who had a thing for women.'' Armistead gave me a mocking leer. ''Sort of a poor man's Dracula, with an extra dose of sexual innuendo. Lots of cleavage.''

Even half asleep, I felt a little foolish that I hadn't picked up this little piece of news on my own. After Yorga's first phone call, I had run his name through a database of historic names without success. With all his name-dropping, I had figured the count to pattern himself from some deceased noble. The idea of checking for celluloid characters hadn't even occurred to me. ''How old were these films?''

''I saw them when I was a kid, and they were already old then.'' Armistead shrugged. ''Sixties, maybe?''

I tried to sort out any implication of the count's newly revealed Hollywood connection, but at this point I wasn't sure it made any difference. I certainly wasn't going to get a chance to quiz the dead bank robber murderer vampire about his taste in films. Still, it was something else to follow up.

Armistead brought the vehicle to a stop in front of the high white front of the Stone River Inn. ''Here we are,'' he said.

I pushed open the door and winced as the cold air swirled into the car. ''Thanks for the lift.''

''Anytime.'' Armistead leaned toward me and smiled hopefully. ''Are you going to be in town long?''

''Only as long as Agent Hoskins makes me stay.'' I slid out of the car and stepped into snow that reached over the top of my low-heeled shoes. I started to close the door, then stopped and leaned back in for a moment. ''And thanks for letting me know about Yorga.''

He grinned. "No problem. I was a vampire nut when I was a kid. Read every book and watched every film that featured fangs." He raised the lapel of his suit coat up to his eyes and peered at me over the edge of the blue material. "I know my bloodsuckers," he said in fine mock-Lugosi.

With my fatigued brain, I couldn't help but laugh. "Please tell me that's not where you learned about porphyria."

" 'Fraid so," Armistead replied. "But don't worry, I've studied up on the syndrome since then. My facts are still good."

"And it's not contagious?"

"Nope," he said. "Like I said, it's an inherited condition. Most cases aren't severe, and when it is severe, it usually strikes children."

"You can't catch it from someone else?" I held out my wounded arm. "Even if you're bitten?"

The mortician's blue eyes widened. He drew back from me into his seat. "Count Yorga bit you?"

His reaction sent a ripple of fear running through me that momentarily banished my thoughts of sleep. I shivered in the cold and nodded. "Yeah."

"How many times?" asked Armistead.

"What?"

He pointed at my arm. "How many times were you bitten?"

"Just once," I answered in a shaking voice.

"Good," said Armistead. "Then you should be safe."

"From the porphyria?"

He shook his head. "No, no. Safe from infcstation by the forces of darkness." He formed a cross with his fingers and held it up to the open car door.

I took a step back. "You don't really believe that."

For just a moment he held the serious expression on his face, then he dissolved into laughter. "Sorry," he sputtered, waving his hands and trying to catch his breath. "If you could only see the expression on your—"

I slammed the door, turned, and stomped up the steps to the Stone River Inn. For a moment I feared the door would be locked. After all, Mrs. Grimes didn't have any guarantee that I would be coming back. But the door opened at my touch.

The long lobby was mostly dark, but there was a single desk lamp burning on the counter. Walking closer, I found an envelope pinned in a circle of light. "Miss McKinnon," said the letters on the side.

The sight of my name gave me a momentary shiver as I recalled Yorga's note back at the diner. But this envelope didn't contain any communications from the undead. Instead it held a brief note from Mrs. Grimes explaining that my things had already been taken up to room four. The room key was in the envelope.

Apparently something had convinced the innkeeper to be helpful. Whatever had brought the change, I was grateful. I stumbled up the stairs, through the door, and dropped everything I was wearing into a heap on the floor. It was not my usual technique to sleep in the buff, but by this point just the idea of unzipping my bag seemed like heavy labor. Thirty second later I was under the sheets and sinking into sleep.

No more than ten seconds after that, I was being shaken awake.

"Stop that," I grumbled. I started to sit up, but my

head seemed to have gained several tons of weight. With Herculean effort, I squeezed open one eyelid. Light. Painfully bright light. Somehow during my ten seconds of sleep, the sun had risen. While I was still trying to make sense of this impossibility, my blurry vision made out the face of Cooper Armistead looking down at me.

I opened my other eye. "What are you doing in my room?"

"Waking you up," he replied with a grin. "Or at least trying to." He had changed into a maroon cable-knit sweater over pleated khaki trousers. Even in my sleep-logged state, I noticed that the clothes were well cut and obviously expensive. I also noticed that the aim of his blue eyes was drifting slowly downward.

It was at about that moment when I remembered that I was *sans* clothing. I snatched at the quilts covering the bed and hugged them against myself. "That doesn't explain what you're doing in here."

Armistead put his hands into his pockets and shrugged. "I just thought this was news you'd want to hear."

"What news?" I asked.

The mortician-to-be raised one eyebrow and gave me a wide grin. "Yorga has risen from his grave."

EIGHT

THE FACE IN THE MIRROR WAS HORRIFYING. SALLOW skin framed bloodshot eyes. Tangled, unwashed hair hung down around a face marked by lack of sleep and traces of unremoved makeup. The teeth were covered in what seemed to be a layer of fur. The *Global Query* had never featured any beast so horrible.

I stuck my tongue out at my reflection, rubbed a damp washcloth across my face, and grabbed a brush out of my purse. Armistead had been nice enough to leave the room so I could get dressed. He hadn't been nice enough to tell me anything more about why he had seen fit to interrupt my all-too-brief sleep. After that single cryptic statement, Armistead had insisted that I would have to come along and see for myself.

With news and people waiting for me downstairs, there wasn't going to be time for luxuries like a shower. The best I could manage was to put my hair back in a loose ponytail, scrape the coating from my teeth, and scrub my pale face until some color returned to my tired cheeks. The results were not impressive. If Cooper Armistead was still making moves on me by the end of the day, he was either interested in my mind or just none too choosy.

My appearance and attitude weren't helped by a return visit from Dante's influenza. The hundred-ton sinus pressure and ripping nasal explosions were not yet in evidence, but there was a sharp ache down in my throat and a pressure in my chest that promised much hacking in my future. All I could hope was that my body would get me through the story before falling apart.

I pulled on a warm teal-colored sweater—being careful not to disturb the bandage on my arm—and slid on a pair of jeans that were, thankfully, a better fit than the ones I had worn on the way into town. With one last scowl at my drawn, gray reflection, I turned and hurried downstairs.

In the lobby of the inn I found not only Cooper Armistead, but also Mrs. Grimes and the round-faced Deputy Doug. There was an interesting array of expressions on their faces. Armistead looked at me with a disturbing eagerness. The deputy appeared to be in a state of confusion that transcended rational thought. Mrs. Grimes was frowning again. For a moment, I thought she was angry, but as I came down the stairs, her expression softened.

"Child," she said in a tone of concern, "you're looking awfully peaked."

I wasn't sure what "peaked" meant, but I was pretty sure it was nothing good. "I'm just tired." I offered up a smile. "Give me a chance to wake up and I'll be fine."

The innkeeper looked at me doubtfully. "Looks to me like you need more time resting."

I silently agreed with her, but if my vampire was up and off his funeral slab, this was definitely not the time to take a break from my story. "I'll be careful," I assured Mrs. Grimes. Then I turned to the others. "All right, can you tell me what's going on?"

Armistead started to answer, but Deputy Doug spoke first. "The sheriff says you're to come back for more questioning."

"Great," I replied. "And what about Yorga? Is he going to be there?"

The deputy blinked and shifted his weight from one foot to another. "You just come with me," he said.

The deputy was so obviously frightened that I resisted my urge to aggravate him further. Instead, I simply nodded. We stepped carefully through the snow along the stone sidewalk and trooped out to a waiting police car, leaving Mrs. Grimes at the top of her stairs. Deputy Doug opened the back door of the police car and gestured for me to get in. Riding in a seat where the door handles had been removed was not in my usual routine, but I went along with it. Armistead followed in his glitzy SUV.

The ride with Deputy Doug was silent but for the chatter of tire chains on the slush-covered highway. I had time to look around the town of Williams Crossing. The neighborhood around the inn was a cluster of homes and small shops that were composed mainly of gray, mortarless stone. The carefully stacked blocks certainly made the buildings look solid, but it also gave them a grim tone. Beyond the village of stone houses, a tall, gothic-revival church loomed over a group of impressive Victorians. Snow dropped from gabled roofs and icicles dangled over covered porches. Wood-frame stores sell-ing hardware, groceries, and enough artwork to stock every loft in Manhattan stood along the main road.

Despite the number of stores, it was clear that Williams Crossing had only one major industry—tourism. Even early on a snowy Sunday morning, there were bundled couples hurrying between shops offering antiques or the output of local artists. Half the cars we passed seemed to be Volvos and every car we passed seemed to be topped with a ski rack. There was a conspicuous lack of fast-food restaurants and chain stores. The whole place was nicely frosted in a fresh coat of fluffy white snow. I would have considered the whole thing quite charming if I hadn't been viewing it through windows covered in wire mesh.

We arrived at the police station and the deputy released me from my moving cell. Inside, I found both Sheriff Loudermilk and Agent Hoskins waiting.

"Well," said the sheriff. He leaned back in his old padded chair and laced his hands together across his stomach. "At least we can still find a reporter when we want one." Loudermilk looked much the same as he had the night before. If anything, he seemed a little amused by the situation.

But if the sheriff was relaxed, Agent Hoskins more than made up for it. The agent's clothing, which had been none too neat to begin with, now looked like it had been slept in, walked on, and used for a dishrag. There was a fresh nest of lines around his eyes, not the worldly lines of experience I had always admired on the face of Jimmy Knowles, but the deep lines of someone under such pressure their skull was in danger of implosion.

Hoskins fixed his wrinkle-rimmed eyes on me. "What do you know about this?" he demanded.

I shrugged. "I don't even know what 'this' is."

The agent's lips pressed together in a snarl. "We'll see about that."

I was starting to feel more than a little irritation of my own. I crossed to the plastic chair in front of Deputy Doug's desk and dropped into it. "If you want my help," I said, "you're going to have to tell me what's going on. Mr. Armistead said something about Yorga, but—"

The sheriff cleared his throat and rocked forward in his swivel chair. "You told us you were a reporter, Miss McKinnon."

I nodded. "That's right."

Loudermilk reached to his desk and picked up a folded pile of off-white sheets. "And would this be your paper?"

There was a horned skull on the front page topped by a banner reading DEVIL'S REMAINS FOUND IN TRAILER PARK. It wasn't hard to identify this classy article as a headliner from the current issue of the *Query*.

"Yeah," I said. "It's not exactly *my* paper, but I do work for them."

"I see." The sheriff peeled off the outer sheets with his big, knuckled hands. "And this story here," he said, putting his finger over the shot of a saber-toothed Yorga stand-in. "This is something you wrote?"

I tried not to wince at the picture as I nodded in agreement. "It's my byline."

"And this . . ." He paused to look at the text. "This count fella in the paper. He's the same as this Willmeyer we had over at the parlor."

"Yes," I said, looking from the sheriff to Agent Hoskins and back again. "I already told both of you all about this."

The two men exchanged a glance. "That's right," replied Hoskins. He folded his arms over his stained trench coat. "But now I'm wondering what next week's story is going to say."

I frowned. "What do you mean?"

The agent walked stiffly over to Loudermilk and pulled the paper from the sheriff's hands. Then he wheeled toward me and waved the pages of the *Query* in my face. "You do pretty good with this vampire shit, don't you, Ms. McKinnon."

I leaned away from the flapping paper. My confusion and annoyance was reaching epic proportions. "What does that have to do with anything?"

Hoskins raised his lip in a sneer. "Just this—don't you think a story about a vampire that gets up from an autopsy table would score with your readers?"

It only took me a couple of seconds to process this question, and once I did, there was no need to answer it. "Yorga's body really is missing."

"As if you don't already know," replied Hoskins. "My men arrived two hours ago and found Willmeyer's body gone."

"And you think I stole the body."

Hoskins scowled even harder than before. "Damn right. You had the opportunity. You had the motive."

I looked around the room. All of them—Sheriff Loudermilk, Deputy Doug, Agent Hoskins, and even Armistead—were looking at me expectantly. I shook my head and tried to keep my anger out of my voice. "I hate to break it to you, but Burke and Hare don't work for the *Global Query*. We may have some questionable stories, but we don't go around stealing bodies—even if it would move some papers.'' I tried to sound as indignant as I could, though the truth was that if Mr. Genovese had been present, lifting the body might well have occured to him.

Hoskins snorted. ''So you admit that Willmeyer's disappearance would boost your sales.''

I gritted my teeth. ''It's a newspaper. Good stories sell papers. A good mass murder would boost sales, but you don't see me carrying a knife.''

''Murder?'' said Sheriff Loudermilk.

I raised my hands. ''It was only an example.'' All right, it was perhaps not the best analogy to make in a police station—especially when I had recently been found in the same room with an all-too-dead body.

Hoskins and the sheriff exchanged another glance. Loudermilk cleared his throat. ''Can you tell us where you were last night, Miss McKinnon?''

For the first time in my life, I wondered what kind of sentence was involved in killing a policeman. ''You know where I was,'' I said slowly and carefully. ''I was here, remember?''

''What about after you left here?'' asked Hoskins. He moved over to stand close to the sheriff. ''Where did you go then?''

I nodded toward Armistead. ''I was lucky enough to get a ride back to the inn.''

The FBI agent nodded. ''And what time did you get to the inn?''

''I'm not sure,'' I said with a shrug. ''Two? Three? You saw me leave.''

''Right,'' agreed Hoskins. ''And what time did you arrive back at the funeral parlor?''

I ran my hand through my hair and tried to think. "I guess it was . . ." I frowned and looked up. "Wait a minute. I didn't go back to the funeral parlor."

Hoskins's mouth stretched in a bitter grin. "I see. Did you have Mr. Armistead remove the body for you?"

"Hey, wait another minute there," said Armistead. "I didn't touch your body." He paused, frowned, and shook his head. "You know what I mean."

Hoskins shrugged. "I know that you had access to the building. And it's obvious you have some connection with Ms. McKinnon."

"I never—" started Armistead.

His protest was interrupted by a buzzing noise that rose from the seemingly limitless depths of the FBI man's wrinkled coat. Agent Hoskins scowled for a moment, then fished in his pocket and produced a shiny black satellite phone. He flipped open the mouthpiece and pressed the device to the side of his shaggy head.

"Hoskins," he barked into the mouthpiece. The agent listened for the space of no more than thirty seconds, but during that time his expression went from anger to surprise to wide-eyed fear.

"Yes," said Hoskins. "Yes. Absolutely." His Adam's apple bobbed in his thick neck. "Yes."

From across the room, Armistead looked my way. His lips moved in a series of words.

I shook my head. "What?" I breathed.

This time the mortician moved his lips with exaggerated slowness. "Looks . . . like . . . the . . . wife . . . is . . . not . . . happy."

It took everything I had not to laugh—a sure sign that exhaustion remained close at hand.

"I understand," Hoskins said in a trembling voice.

"Right away." He lowered the phone from his ear and stared across the room with a stunned gaze.

"Agent Hoskins?" I called softly. "Are you all right?"

Hoskins nodded. "No . . . I mean, yes. Yes, I'm fine." He jammed the phone back into his pocket and drew in a ragged breath. Then he turned toward me. "Ms. McKinnon."

"Yes?"

"Do you remember when I suggested you should stay in town?"

I nodded. "Yeah."

"Good," said Hoskins. He walked over to the door and stood looking out at the snowy New England landscape. "I think you should consider it more than a suggestion—for your own sake." He looked around at Sheriff Loudermilk. "You men might consider taking Ms. McKinnon into custody. Protective custody."

The sincerity of the agent's tone sent chills down my back that had nothing to do with the snow outside. "What do you mean?" I asked. "Protection from what?" Now it was my voice that was shaking.

The FBI agent didn't reply. He simply pulled his trench coat closed, stepped past me and Armistead, and pushed open the front door. There was a momentary swirl of cold air that sent papers fluttering from the desks. Then the door slammed and Hoskins walked away along the snowy sidewalk.

Deputy Doug frowned like a four-year-old deprived of ice cream. "Where's he going? He didn't even arrest anybody."

"Looks like he's walking south," answered Sheriff

Loudermilk. ''Expect he'll keep it up until he reaches his car or runs out of road.''

I ignored the sheriff's attempt at humor and watched Hoskins through the foggy windows. The agent walked quickly with his face tilted down and his shoulders hunched against the wind. He passed a tall red brick church, paused for a moment in the shadow of the building's tall spire, then disappeared around the corner.

I turned back to face Loudermilk. ''Now what?'' I asked.

The sheriff shrugged. ''Hard to say. From what the coroner reported, I have no murder to worry about.'' He rubbed the gray stubble on his chin. ''Of course, old Armistead never does much to the ones we send him. Still, I expect he knows dead when he sees it.''

''I think I can certify that Mr. Willmeyer was indeed dead,'' said Armistead the younger. ''It didn't take an autopsy to see that.''

''Maybe you should have done a little cutting,'' replied the sheriff. ''Maybe then the body wouldn't have wandered away.'' He stared off into space for a few moments and sucked his thin cheeks in against his teeth. He turned his gray eyes on me. ''I guess you best follow the agent's advice. I don't know about this protective custody bit, but for now you don't leave Williams Crossing.''

''How long is now?'' I asked.

Sheriff Loudermilk's lips curled in an expression that just might have been a smile. ''Till you're told otherwise.''

It wasn't what I wanted to hear. United Airlines was expecting me on an afternoon flight back to St. Louis, and Bill Genovese was expecting me back at the *Query* bright and early the next morning—complete with a story on my interview with Count Yorga. Finding out that his vampire was dead and his reporter was stuck in Vermont was not likely to make Mr. Genovese very pleasant. Somehow, I didn't think arguing with the sheriff was going to change his mind. I looked at Armistead. "Would you give me another ride? I need to get to my car."

The mortician's smile was much easier to read. "Gladly," he said. "I'll take you anywhere you want to go."

"To my car would be fine." I bid as polite a farewell as I could manage to the sheriff and moonfaced Deputy Doug. A minute later I was once again wrapped in the padded seat of Armistead's luxury four-wheeler on my way back to the Stone River Inn.

"Now that you're forced to stay in our fair city," said my driver, "how are you going to pass your time?"

I had no doubt that Cooper Armistead had some ideas about how we might spend the tedious hours between now and the time when I was permitted to leave Williams Crossing, but I had my own notions of something to while away the time. As far as I could see, I had two immediate problems: I needed a story, and I needed to get home. The cause for both problems was Yorga's untimely demise. There seemed to be only one cure.

"I'm going to find the body," I announced.

Armistead took his eyes off the snowy road and stared at me. "What?"

I nodded. "I'm going to find the body, and then I'm going to get out of town."

"But how?" asked the mortician. "I mean, Hoskins

is with the FBI. If he can't find the body, how can you?''

I smiled. ''The FBI might be the world's greatest police force, but when it comes to finding the weird stuff, the *Global Query* is completely out of this world.''

THE POPULATION OF THE BASEMENT AT ARMISTEAD AND Sons had been cut in half since my visit.

"What happened to all your customers?" I asked, waving a hand at the empty tables.

"Two of them are upstairs for viewings," explained Cooper. "And, well, you already know about the other."

I nodded and moved over to the table where Yorga's body had been lying. There were various pale stains on the steel surface, all of which I was sure came from assorted unpleasant sources. I made no claim to be a great detective, but unless Yorga's skills included post-mortem invisibility, he was almost certainly missing. "Tell me what happened here last night."

Cooper shook his head and jammed his hands into the pockets of his admirably snug trousers. "I wasn't lying back at the station. I really don't know where the body went."

"I'm not talking about that," I said. I bent low over

the brushed steel table. ''I'm talking about what happened when Hoskins's men got here. Did you see them?''

''Oh. Yeah. Yeah, I did.''

I turned my head to look at him, holding my hair away from the stained table with one hand. ''So what did you think of the G-men?''

Cooper considered this for a moment, his blue eyes focused on the ceiling. ''They weren't even men,'' he said. ''Or at least, not all men. There were four of them here when I got back from taking you to the Stone River. Two men and two women.''

''Notice anything in particular about them?'' I asked as I stood up straight.

Cooper grinned. ''One of the women was really quite attractive.''

I should have known this would be the first thing he remembered. ''Anything else?'' I asked around a frown. ''Anything with a little more meaning?''

''Like what?''

''Like what did they do? Did you talk to them?''

Cooper shrugged. ''I didn't really get a chance to talk. They were all wearing masks, so they—''

''Wait a second,'' I interjected. ''They were all what?''

''Wearing masks.'' Cooper cupped his hand over his mouth and nose. ''Biological protective masks,'' he said, his voice muffled by his fingers. ''Good ones, with multilevel filters and auxiliary air supplies.''

I walked slowly around the room and stared at him across a sheet-wrapped body. ''You're kidding.''

Cooper shook his head. ''Nope. And they were dressed in hazard suits.''

For several seconds, I couldn't think of what to say. The vision of Agent Hoskins went through my mind. I remembered the mask and heavy gloves he had pulled out before handling Yorga's body. It had seemed like a needless precaution at the time, but if the whole team had come wearing gear suitable for tackling an outbreak of Ebola, maybe there really was something worth worrying about. A little shivery feeling began to work at the base of my spine—like an ice cube that someone had slipped into my top while I wasn't looking.

"Why didn't you tell me about this before?" I asked.

The mortician-in-training shrugged and leaned back against a shelf loaded with industrial-sized jars of foundation. "There wasn't much time," he said. "I thought the important thing was that the body was missing."

I nodded. "I'll give you that much. Missing vampire bodies go right to the top of my list." I picked up a bent, sharply pointed tool from a tray beside the table. It was shiny, had a crook in the center, and I had no idea of either its name or its purpose. "But," I said, shaking the toothy instrument for emphasis, "for future reference, any time you see people walking around in space suits, please bring it to my attention."

"They weren't space suits," he started. "They were more—"

I whacked the shiny tool against the side of the metal table. The sound it made was louder than I expected, but it served to stop Cooper's words. "Close enough," I said. "Did any of them say why they were wearing all this gear? Do you know what they were afraid of?"

Cooper shook his head. "Like I said, porphyria is an inherited syndrome. No one could catch it. I figured they were just being overly cautious."

I turned the unnamed instrument over in my hands and tried to think. For my own sake, I hoped that Cooper was right. "What about the death certificate? Was there anything on there that might have hinted at a communicable disease?"

Cooper gave a short laugh. "Hardly. My father was never very creative when it came to things like that. I'm sure that if he told the police it was a heart attack, that's what he put down on the certificate."

I looked down again at the stained table where Yorga's body had lain. If he really was infected, the little pink spots on the steel might hold enough virus to wipe out a room full of investigative reporters and a few morticians on the side. Worse, all the blood—and other fluids—left behind at the Stone River Inn might be swimming with infection waiting to chow down on Mrs. Grimes and her guests. Worst of all was the wound in my arm. If anything had infected Yorga, then whole fleets of disease were almost surely cruising around my blood system.

As if just thinking about it was enough to activate a malicious bacteria, my arm began to pound. I moved a visit to a real doctor way up my list of things to do in the immediate future. In fact, it was only one slot short of my top priority.

But first I had to figure out what was going on.

"How did he know?" I asked.

"What?"

I stared into Cooper's blue eyes. "Hoskins. The first thing he did when we got here was put on a mask. What made him think he needed to do that?"

Cooper shrugged. "Your vampire guy looked pretty ill. Maybe it was just a precaution."

"Maybe," I agreed. "But how did he know to bring a mask and gloves in the first place? I mean, I doubt Sheriff Loudermilk gave a detailed description when the state agents called. All Hoskins knew was that a bank robber had died from a heart attack. So why the mask?"

"Standard procedure?" offered Cooper.

I shook my head. "Somehow I don't believe every FBI agent runs around with gloves and a mask in their pocket. Hoskins showed up out of nowhere, and I think he had a pretty good idea what he was going to find. The question is, how?"

Evidently, neither of us had an easy answer to that one. We stood in silence for long moments, sharing the solitude with the remaining corpses. In one of the viewing rooms overhead, an organ began to play. Filtered through the floorboards of the mortuary, nothing but the lowest notes remained. Surrounded by dead bodies, the effects of the faint, broken bass line was enough to make goose bumps break out on my arms. I dropped the gleaming instrument onto the not-so-gleaming table and put my hand over my mouth to stifle a cough. "Come on," I said. "Let's get out of here."

I followed Cooper up the stairs. At the top, I started to turn back to the lobby, but the young mortician grabbed me by the arm.

"Let's go this way," he said, nodding toward a smaller hallway. "Otherwise you'll have to shake hands with a room full of grieving relatives."

The path he had chosen led away from the crowds and into a room full of coffins laid out on cloth-covered stands. The oblong boxes displayed surprising variety, ranging from polished black wood that would have looked at home in another century, to round-shouldered shells formed from oddly tinted metal alloys. In all, there had to be at least a dozen coffins laid out in two rows. "Wow," I said, looking at the display. "Did you guys have a plane crash in the area?"

"Oh, these aren't occupied at the moment," said Cooper. He reached to the side of a shiny silver box with gold-tone handles and flipped up the top to reveal an interior lined in plush blue velvet. "This is the display room. This is where we bring the teary-eyed widows to sucker them into putting a dozen grand into the ground."

I looked at the line of boxes and wrinkled my nose. "With a sales pitch like that, I can see how you do so well."

Cooper's lips tightened into an oddly humorless smile. "Dear," he said, "I can see that this has hurt you terribly. Terribly. But you have just one more decision to make. It's time for you to buy the last thing you will ever buy for your loved one on this Earth."

His voice had taken on a quality that was an eerie mixture of sympathy, grief, and a brand of infinite resignation. The combination was enough to make me shudder. "All right," I admitted. "You are better at it than I thought." Another cough jerked out of my lungs and escaped before I could cover my mouth. In the silent room, it seemed as loud as a cannon shot. I felt a little dizzy for a moment, and had to lean against the nearest coffin while I caught my breath.

Cooper started toward me. "Are you okay?" he asked.

I nodded and took my hands away from the cold brass top of the coffin. "I'm fine. Come on, let's get out of here before you really start to give me a sales pitch."

We sneaked quietly out of the building and emerged in the parking lot. Overhead, the sky was once again gray and lowering, with a few thin flurries adding a fresh crust to the snow that had fallen overnight. Even so, after being in the dimly lit funeral home, I found the brightness of the winter day almost too much to bear. I squinted hard against the blinding glare and fumbled my way toward the cars.

"Where to now?" Cooper asked as we reached the door of his SUV.

No easy answer to that question sprang to mind. Yorga was dead, his body missing. Agent Hoskins was gone. There was nothing left in Williams Crossing but a lot of quaint shops and tourists on their way back from a weekend on the ski slopes. "Let's head for the inn," I said at last. "The murder scene was there. Maybe we can find something." It wasn't a great idea, but at least it was an idea.

Cooper came around and opened my door. I was about to climb inside when I noticed that he was looking at me with a frown.

"What's wrong?" I asked.

"Nothing. I mean, it's just that . . ." He stopped and shrugged. "You don't look so good."

I almost laughed. Almost. This was not the kind of comment I appreciated from attractive men—or anyone else. "I don't feel so good, either."

"No," said Cooper. "I guess not." He looked at me with concern for a moment longer. "Maybe when we get out to the Stone River, you should lie down for awhile."

"That would be nice," I agreed, "but I have work to

do.'' I put my hand over another cough. ''Come on. Let's get out of here.''

I slipped inside and I sank gratefully into the soft leather seat of the Mercedes. I glanced over at Cooper as he joined me and shut his door. ''I appreciate your chauffeuring me around.''

''No problem.'' He looked at me and grinned. ''I've enjoyed every minute of it.'' Despite his previous comment on my current appearance, I could tell there was still something more than friendly interest in his expression. ''I was just down here from school for the weekend, and I expected to be bored straight through to Monday.''

This time I did laugh. ''Glad to know I helped break the tedium of your life.''

Cooper put the vehicle into gear. We were halfway across the parking lot when he suddenly stopped and turned toward me with an odd expression. ''Why did you call it that?''

I frowned. ''Call what what?''

''The Stone River Inn,'' he said. ''You called it the murder scene.''

''Yeah.''

''But there was no murder. Yorga—I mean Willmeyer—died of a heart attack, or from some complication of his condition.''

''Ahh,'' I said with a confidence I didn't feel. ''That's what *they* want you to think.''

Cooper frowned. ''They who?''

''When you work for the *Global Query,*'' I explained, ''you find that there is always a 'they.' ''

''Do you really think Count Yorga was murdered?''

"I don't—" I started, then I stopped and nodded. "Yeah. Yeah, I think maybe I do."

Cooper took a deep breath. "Do you think you should go explain this theory to the sheriff?"

"Not at the moment," I said. "I have no evidence. More importantly, I have no story." I pointed at the slush-edged road ahead. "That's why we have to get back to the inn."

"But if someone has really been killed," he said, "don't you think contacting the police is a wise idea?"

The question made me feel more amused than it should—a sure sign that I had gone way too long without sleep. "Why?" I asked. "Are you afraid to go back out there? Don't you want a little excitement?"

He shook his head. "Not really. Okay, there's excitement, which is great. And then there's danger. I'm definitely against the danger thing."

I smiled at him and shook my head. "I'll keep that in mind. If the bad guys put a gun to my head, I won't count on you for rescue."

"Hey," said Cooper. "If you think bad guys are going to put a gun to your head, my suggestion is to take your head somewhere else." He turned a corner and waved at a pair of kids coming down the sidewalk with a sled in tow. "It's just hard for me to think of any place in Williams Crossing as being actually dangerous."

I stared out the car window at the rows of buildings sliding past. There were neat brick-and-frame houses mixed in with an architecture lesson's worth of styles. A tall, Gothic Revival church dominated one corner, while a stern clapboard-sided academy loomed over the next. There were cupolas and verandahs and corner towers that rose high over the street. The scene was spoiled a bit by the brown snow that had been piled up along the road by snowplows, but I could still imagine Curier and Ives putting a frame around the place and capturing it for future generations of holiday mugs and place mats.

Despite the postcard-worthy nature of my surroundings, I wasn't feeling much like a happy camper. I was sick, my contact was dead, and somebody was lying to me. Something was definitely rotten in the humble village of Williams Crossing. In fact, several somethings were wrong. First off, Hoskins had appeared without warning and taken over the investigation without so much as an excuse me. Usually, the FBI didn't come into a local jurisdiction without fourteen kinds of paperwork and a special request, but no one—not even me—had thought to protest his right to take over. His actions clearly showed that he had been expecting some sort of disease or toxin, but he had done nothing to warn any bystanders that they might be in danger. None of it, from beginning to end, was even close to what I regarded as typical FBI behavior.

As Cooper and I rolled slowly through this winter wonderland, I bit my lip and tried to think of my next move. The room at the Stone River Inn might provide some insight, but it wasn't likely. I was in serious need of an additional information source. It was Sunday morning, so the *Global Query* offices were closed—not that I could count on any of my colleagues to provide research without stealing the story—and the Stone River Inn didn't exactly look like the sort of place that had Internet terminals in every room. Usually, this was the kind of situation where I might try to drag Jimmy into the picture, but considering the way we had left things back in St. Louis, calling Jimmy for help on my story didn't seem like such a great idea.

Then an idea occurred to me. "Does this thing have a phone?" I asked.

Cooper raised one eyebrow. "But of course," he said, heaping on an accent appropriate for handing out imported mustard. With a deft move, he flipped open a small compartment, extracted a slim digital phone, and presented it to me.

"Thanks." I dialed from memory and waited out a long series of rings before the phone at the other end was fumbled off the hook.

"This is the *Journal,*" growled a deep voice. "We're closed. Call back tomorrow."

A cough with poor timing bubbled up my throat. I held the speaker away from my face until the fit had passed, then scrambled to get out an answer before it was too late. "Wait," I called into the tiny mouthpiece. "Shaver! Don't hang up."

There was a full ten seconds of silence from the other end before the voice came again. "Is that you, McKinnon?"

I was a little surprised that Shaver had recognized my voice, but that didn't mean I was pleased. Shaver Wilcox had been at the *Green County Journal* since newspapers were inscribed in soft clay and baked into tablets. All those years had given him a great familiarity with the *Journal*'s archaic equipment. It had not given him a heart warm enough to melt a snowflake.

"It's me," I agreed reluctantly.

"Well then," he snarled, "you don't want to be calling. Jimmy's not here."

That was a surprise. Sunday was the day the *Journal*

cranked the presses for the weekly edition. Keeping Jimmy away when the presses were rolling usually took at least three major crises and a team of wild mules. "Is he all right?" I asked.

Shaver was slow to answer. "Fine as he ever was, I suppose. But he's not here, so you—"

"That's okay," I interjected. "I wasn't calling for Jimmy."

This time I could almost feel the puzzlement humming over the phone line. "Then what do you want?" asked Shaver.

"I want to talk to Jen."

Shaver made a noise low in his throat. "You leave that girl alone. She's not after your boy."

I glanced over at Cooper. He was driving on along the slush-covered road, apparently oblivious to my embarrassing conversation. "Look," I whispered into the phone. "I'm not concerned about that."

"What?" said Shaver. "I can't hear you."

I scowled and raised my voice slightly. "I said I'm not afraid that—"

"What?"

"I'm not worried about her stealing Jimmy!" I shouted. "Just put her on." While I waited, I could hear Cooper chuckling under his breath from the other side of the car. I did my best to ignore him.

"Hello?" said a nervous but still bouncy voice on the phone. "Ms. Skye?"

I could have corrected her again about calling me by my pen name, but I make it a special point to avoid lecturing people when I'm about to ask them for favors. "Savvy," I said. "Just call me Savvy."

The sound of my voice seemed to reassure the teenager. "Hi, Savvy," she said brightly. "What's up?"

"I need help."

"With a story?" asked Jen.

"Yes."

"Cool!" There was a rustling of paper and the squeak of unoiled coasters. I could picture Jen settling herself over one of the ancient, scarred desks at the *Journal* with pencil in hand. "What do you need?" she asked eagerly.

The girl's quick willingness to help was enough to make me almost dizzy. Jen didn't ask about bylines, or pay, or give an excuse. I decided that I very much liked having a fan. She might be unforgivably pretty, but I was willing to let even that slide for the moment.

"I need you to check on a couple of names for me," I said.

"Right," Jen replied. "Go ahead."

"The first one is Frank Hoskins," I said, pronouncing the name carefully. "He's supposed to be an FBI agent, but I can't be sure. Probably lives somewhere on the East Coast."

"Frank Hoskins," she repeated. "Okay, but how am I supposed to find him?"

"Any way you want," I replied. "Check the net. Run a people search. Try Nexus, Lexus, and any other 'us you can think of."

" 'Kay."

"Good. The next one is Michael Willmeyer. You should be able to find about him on the FBI's site."

I could hear the clatter of computer keys. Evidently Jen had wasted no time in putting the web to work. "Got it," she said. "Anything else?"

"Not right now." I smiled at the phone. "Thanks, Jen. I really appreciate this."

"No biggie," the girl replied quickly. "This is exciting."

I almost laughed. Maybe there had been a time when I loved trolling the net for the occasional nibble of fact. It was hard to remember. Only a couple of years on the job and not having acheived the credibility I sought, I was already starting to think of myself as the cynical hard-bitten reporter. I hoped Jen would still find the task exciting after spending hours slogging through unrelated data. "Do what you can," I said. "I'll call back in a couple of hours."

" 'Kay," said Jen. "And Savvy?"

"Yeah?"

"You remember what I said about Jimmy?"

"Um, not really."

"Well, I was right."

I frowned at the phone. "What do you mean?" I asked. But it was too late. I was talking to nothing but static. I hung up and passed the phone back to Cooper. He took the small device and stowed it away.

"Your assistant?" he asked.

"Not quite."

I wondered for a moment about Jen's last statement. It seemed to me that she had said a lot of things about Jimmy during our last encounter. Which part of her little pep talk had come to pass was unclear. One thing was certain—it would have to wait until I could manage an escape from Williams Crossing.

In the meantime I wasn't really sure how much I could count on Jen to do my cyberwork, but getting her to chase after Hoskins and Willmeyer made me feel like I was at least taking some action. Ever since this thing started, I had been letting other people run the show.

Mr. Genovese had forced me into the assignment, Hoskins and Sheriff Loudermilk had danced me around, and the count had the poor graces to get me into a mess by dying. If I was going to get out of Williams Crossing with a story in hand—and without finding out where the town locked away its rare miscreants—I was going to have to take charge of my situation.

"It's time I put the bite on this vampire story," I muttered under my breath.

"What?" said Cooper.

I pointed at the snowy road ahead. "Drive on, Van Helsing. Daylight is fading and the castle draws near."

TEN

NO SOONER DID THE HIGH GAMBREL ROOF OF THE STONE River Inn come into view than I felt an overwhelming wave of sleepiness. No matter how many vampires and FBI agents were missing, no matter how badly I needed a story, nothing sounded so good to me as five, or ten, or maybe twenty hours of nice, uninterrupted sleep. I stretched my arms up over my head and fought back a yawn.

''Home again, home again,'' said Cooper as he turned off the main street.

''Please,'' I replied. ''Let's hope it's not my home for much longer.''

Cooper made an overdramatic gasp. ''You say that as if you're not enjoying your stay in our fair city.''

''I'm sure Williams Crossing is a blast and a half,'' I replied. ''But I generally find myself more comfortable in towns where the sheriff hasn't ordered me to stay.''

The Mercedes crunched up the snow-covered driveway of the Stone River Inn and pulled in behind my rental car. I climbed out quickly and leaned back through the door to thank Cooper, but when I looked in I found he was already on his way out the other side.

"You don't have to come," I said. "I've taken up enough of your weekend."

Cooper laughed. "Believe me, I don't mind." He shut his door and put his hands in the pockets of his khaki slacks. "If it's all the same to you, I'll come along and help you crack the case, Ms. Holmes."

Normally, I didn't like the idea of anyone following me around on a story, but since Cooper was both familiar with the locals and painfully attractive, I decided to relax my normal rules. Two days was not exactly long enough to scrub Jimmy out of my head—or heart—and I wasn't feeling terrifically romantic, but Cooper was something of an ego boost. The fact that he was still willing to follow me around, despite my current run in with the super flu, was definitely flattering.

"I thought you were just in town for a few days," I said. "I wouldn't want to keep you from visiting with your family."

"No thanks," replied Cooper with a shake of his head. "If I go home, my dad will just put me to work painting eyebrows on old Mrs. Gively." He shivered. "That's a family experience I can do without."

I started to laugh, but it turned into a cough that left me leaning against the car. "Yeah, well," I said once I had gathered my breath. "I'm not sure hanging around with me is going to be much more fun than taking care of your father's customers."

To my great disappointment, Cooper didn't laugh at this little joke. "How are you feeling?" he asked, surveying me critically. "You look . . ."

His voice trailed away, but that didn't stop me from scowling. The flattering quotient generated by the attention of a good-looking, wealthy man was being seriously eroded. "If you're about to tell me how bad I look again, maybe you really should go paint those eyebrows," I suggested.

"You don't look bad, exactly. Just . . ." He paused and shrugged. "Pale."

Pale wasn't exactly a compliment, but it could definitely be worse. I suppose that next to Cooper's San Tropez bronze, my skin would look a bit blanched—neither Vermont nor St. Louis offered many opportunities for frolicking in the winter sun. And my fight with the flu was probably doing nothing for my complexion. Of all the things he could have said, I could live with pale.

Without further discussion, I picked up my purse, gathered the remains of my ego, and went up the steps to the Stone River Inn with Cooper following two steps behind.

Coarse crystals of milky salt crunched under my feet and a wind chime made from copper vanes sounded the notes of a chill breeze as I stepped onto the porch. The white winter sun and its reflection from the snow filled the scene with so much light, it was painful. I pulled the edges of my coat tight, squinted against the glare, and hurried across the boards toward the green-trimmed front door.

Before I could reach for the knob, the door swung open and Mrs. Grimes stood framed against the glowing wood of the lobby. "You've missed breakfast," she announced in a sharp tone.

If the reception I had received the night before was

arctic, and the send-off that morning somewhat thawed, it was immediately obvious that some new factor had tipped Mrs. Grimes's attitude back to the frosty side of the thermostat.

"What's wrong?" I asked.

Mrs. Grimes shook her head. "Nothing," she said with a sniff. "Not a thing, but that all my guests are gone."

I winced. "Look, I'm really sorry," I replied. "Was it all the noise last night?"

The innkeeper folded her arms over her ample chest. "Oh, last night was just the start of it. My last two guests left after those people in the plastic suits came charging in."

"They're here?" I stood on tiptoe and tried to see over Mrs. Grimes. I saw no sign of an FBI team in hazardous-environment gear.

Mrs. Grimes gave a harumph that was nearly a growl. "They've already left." She waved an arm at the staircase. "And they took half the furniture with them."

"The furniture?" I squeezed around the innkeeper and looked up the stairs. "Why would they take furniture?"

"I'm afraid they didn't consult me," said Mrs. Grimes. "Didn't even offer to pay."

I started up the staircase. "They must have thought there was something in the room connected with the murder."

"Murder!" squawked the innkeeper. Her eyes widened dramatically behind her wire-rimmed glasses. "You mean that man was murdered in my inn?"

"Sorry," I said quickly. "Slip of the tongue." I hurried up the rest of the stairs to find the door to the room where I had met Yorga crisscrossed by bands of yellow-and-black police tape. The tape hadn't been there the night before. Either the Williams Crossing police had paid a visit while I wasn't looking, or the mysterious space-suit squad had wanted to keep people away from the scene of Yorga's death.

It worked for a good ten seconds. Then I reached out for the doorknob and gave it a twist. Whoever had put the tape over the door had apparently trusted in the strips of plastic to deter any visitors—the door was not locked. It swung smoothly into the room, revealing a bed that had been stripped down to a feather mattress and a bare floor spotted with sunlight shining through the irregular windows.

I pushed aside the strips of tape and stepped into the room. There was a faint, stringent smell somewhere between bleach and rubbing alcohol hovering in the air. The small table that had been in the room the previous night was missing. So was the lamp. And the chair. And the rugs. Even the curtains over the high, narrow windows had been taken.

"I think they meant for you to stay outside," Cooper said from the doorway.

I nodded without looking around. "I took that as a suggestion."

"Uh-huh." The leather heels of Cooper's shoes clacked against the bare boards as he walked slowly into the room. "I think Mrs. Grimes is downstairs calling the police. They might think you should take these suggestions more seriously."

I took a moment to think about the possible legal implications then shook my head. "I have a reservation in this inn—to this room, in fact—so I don't think they'll be able to get me for trespassing. And the tape only says 'police.' '' I shrugged. ''They'll have a hard time finding a charge.''

''Maybe.'' Cooper sat down on the edge of the bare mattress and pulled off his coat. ''Don't blame me if they put you away for a few days while they think about it.''

Looking at him sitting in his shirtsleeves made me start to feel a bit warmer myself. I opened the front of my wool coat and let it gape over the top and jeans I had hastily thrown on that morning. ''The FBI and the local police have both told me not to leave town; I'm already about as put away as I can get. Let's look around while we can.''

''Look for what?'' Cooper raised his hands and waved them at the almost-empty room. ''What do you expect to find?''

''I'm not sure.'' I crouched near the place where I had held Yorga in his death throes. ''There has to be some clue.''

''Clue?'' Cooper said with a hint of laughter in his voice. ''Something like Count Yorga in the bedroom with a candlestick?''

''Yes,'' I said, with growing irritation. ''Something like that.''

''Then you really do think this was a murder?''

I stopped staring at the room and tried to put my thoughts in order. ''I think the FBI wouldn't have come here if they didn't consider this an important scene. And they wouldn't have taken the furniture if they didn't think what happened in this room was worth investigating.''

Cooper nodded. "Like perhaps the death of a wanted criminal?"

"Like the *murder* of a wanted criminal," I insisted. "If Yorga had just dropped from a heart attack, I hardly think they'd be tearing up the room where he fell."

Cooper considered this for a moment, then shrugged. "Okay. So maybe they did think the circumstances were . . . suspicious."

I turned around slowly and frowned at the bare floor and exposed windows. "Something was here," I said. "Something important enough to clean out the room."

" 'Was' is the operative word. Whatever it was, it's gone now." Cooper stood up and flicked a lock of black hair away from his eyes. "How about leaving while we can still do it under our own power?"

I turned slowly around, making a survey of the room. Hoskins's crew had left very little to work with. Even the stains on the floor where the count had bled out his weird pink and violet blood had been scrubbed until the wood was spotless. It seemed that Cooper was right. If this room was a crime scene, it was a crime scene where all traces of the crime had been removed.

A tap at the window made me jump. I spun about and saw that there were no vampires hovering outside the glass. The brisk winter wind was driving the snow-frosted limb of a maple tree against the window. Even in the daylight the sound of the leafless twigs being drawn across the panes was enough to raise goose bumps. This combined with the breeze leaking in around the window made me develop a serious bout of shivers.

"Maybe we should go talk to Mrs. Grimes," Cooper suggested. "She could at least give you an idea of what was taken."

I nodded. ''That sounds like a . . . a good . . .''

It was that chill breeze that made me pause. This wasn't just a cold spot, this was an actual movement of icy air through the cleaned-out room—not something I expected to feel in the *This Old House* cum Donna Reed confines of the Stone River Inn. I wondered for a moment if Yorga might have cracked opened the window. He had been an odd enough character. Maybe a little ice-cold air had been to his liking. Or maybe the FBI agents had opened a window while stealing the curtains.

I took a step toward the window, intending to check the latch, but a closer inspection showed that this breeze would not be stopped so easily. Two of the window's tall, rippled panes of glass had been broken—or, more accurately, punctured. Three small holes, each no bigger around than the tip of a ballpoint pen, penetrated the glass of one pane. A fourth opening had been made though the pane just above. Each of the holes was precise and neat, as if drilled by some tiny auger.

I reached out to touch the gleaming edge of one small hole then hesitated at the last moment. ''Cooper?''

''What?''

I brought my face close to the glass, watching sunlight glitter in the quartet of openings. ''When the body came in to your father, did he do any tests?''

Cooper stepped closer. ''What kind of tests?'' he asked. ''Did you find something?''

''Yes,'' I replied. The word came out in a puff of vapor as it struck the jets of cold air passing through the glass. ''Did they run any blood tests? Toxicology tests?''

''Toxicology? I doubt it. My dad wouldn't order those unless he had a reason.'' Cooper leaned down at my side, putting his hands on the knees of his crisply pressed trousers. ''Hey, where did those holes come from?''

''That's what we have to find out.'' I stood up straight. ''If I wanted some tests run, do you know someone who could do them?''

''I guess,'' Cooper replied, still looking at the perforated glass. ''But what are we going to test? Your vampire has already vanished with the morning light.''

I smiled and reached down for Cooper's hand. ''Follow me.''

We walked quickly out of the room where Yorga had breathed his last and stepped across the well-buffed boards to the room where Mrs. Grimes had moved my things the night before. I reached down beside the bed, and picked up a crumpled mass and held it up.

''Run tests on this,'' I said.

Cooper pulled his fingers free of my grip and took a half-step back, his nose wrinkled in disgust. ''What's that?''

''The sweater I was wearing last night.'' I extended the damp, matted clothing. ''Yorga threw up on me while he was dying. I think he threw up blood.''

''How . . . wonderful.'' Cooper took hold of the soiled garment with two fingers and held it out at arm's length. ''What do you want me to have it tested for?''

I shrugged. ''Anything. Everything.''

''You might have to be a little more specific,'' he suggested. ''Unless you want to give me a week and a stack of cash.''

''You've seen plenty of dead bodies,'' I replied. ''Go with your instincts.''

Cooper laughed. ''My instincts are to burn this

sweater and wash my hand in a gallon of bleach. But I'll give it a shot.''

''Wonderful.'' I favored him with what I hoped was a winning smile. ''I appreciate this.''

''Really?'' He raised an eyebrow. ''Are you grateful enough to join me for dinner?''

One day's acquaintance was enough to know that Cooper Armistead was hoping for something more than shared subsistence, but I trusted myself to fend off any overt advances. Besides, I needed the tests. ''Dinner sounds fine,'' I replied. ''If you find something I'll even pay for the meal.''

He gave a little mocking sigh. ''I would never ask a lady to pay for a meal.''

Whether it was sexism, or merely misguided gallantry, I was sure Mr. Genovese and the *Global Query*'s minuscule travel budget would be relieved. ''Fine,'' I said. ''You pay, I'll eat.'' I put my hand against his hard, flat chest and pushed him gently out onto the balcony that ran around the top of the lobby stairs. ''Now go see what you can find.''

''What are you going to do while I run tests?'' he asked as he backed through the door.

''Don't worry,'' I said. ''I'll stay busy.''

Cooper gave a last, disgusted look to the sodden sweater in his grip, then turned to walk down the stairs.

I was about to leave on an errand of my own when the phone began to chime. It took me a second to locate the instrument, which was sitting on the floor near the corner of the room. I stared at it for the space of two more rings, then walked across to it quickly and lifted the handset from the cradle.

''Hello?''

Even over the phone line, it was easy to identify Mrs. Grimes's disgusted grunt. "I thought you would still be in there. Hold on, you have a call."

"Who is—" I started, but before I could finish there was a loud click and a sudden hollowness on the phone.

"Savvy Skye," I said cautiously. This time, at least, I remembered my pen name.

"Savvy!" cried an excited voice over the line. "I found what you wanted."

"Jen? Is that you?"

"Uh-huh."

"And you already found something on the net?" I asked in surprise. I had expected the search to take much longer.

"Oh, yeah," the teenager replied with breathless enthusiasm. "See, I talked to Craig—he's in my algebra class—and Craig, he talked to Dave and they—"

"Tell me that part later," I said as strongly as I could manage without offending Jen. "Right now, I just need to know what you found out."

The girl was silent for a moment. "Okay," she said at last. "There wasn't much on the first guy. I've got some matches on the name, but it's with a big drug company, not the FBI. Can't tell if it's the same guy."

"Probably not. Hoskins is a fairly common name." That was disappointing news. It seemed that good old Agent Hoskins was not going to surface easily. "What about Willmeyer?" I asked.

"He's the one I found," Jen replied. "His information was right where you said it would be."

"The FBI data?"

"Yeah." There was a slight delay. "Willmeyer, Michael J. Age 42, height 5' 10" . . ."

The description sounded close enough. I suppose it was no surprise that they'd failed to mention the white, blotched skin or the pale, wild hair. "Does it say what he did?" I asked.

"Uh-huh," said Jen. "Special Agent. I found his name in a list of awards."

For a moment I only frowned at the phone. Then what she had said began to sink in. "That's not right."

"What's not right?" asked Jen. "It all came straight from the printout."

"Well, something's messed up," I insisted. "It's Hoskins who's an FBI agent, not Willmeyer."

"No," said a voice from the door.

I looked up to see a bulky figure blocking the light from the doorway. "Who are you?" I asked in a shaky voice.

The figure stepped into the room and I saw that it was the fat man from the plane. A moment after that, I saw the gun in his hand. He ran a blunt finger down the glossy chrome barrel of his gun and smiled at me. "Willmeyer was, in fact, a very good agent," he said. "It's Hoskins you should worry about."

ELEVEN

LESS THAN AN HOUR BEFORE, I HAD BEEN THINKING OF myself as a jaded, hard-bitten reporter. But jaded did not include a casual attitude about people waving pistols in my vicinity.

Without thinking, I made a frightened squeak and took a step back. The base of the phone slid from the table and crashed to the floor. I managed to keep my grip on the handset, from which the distant voice of Jen could be heard calling with increasing alarm.

The fat man stepped into the room and gestured with the dark barrel of his gun. ''You might do well to stay back from those windows,'' he suggested in a mild tone. ''As I think you already know, a proximity to that view proved unhealthy for your friend Willmeyer.''

I licked my lips and swallowed the lump in my throat. ''At the moment I'm more worried about the guns inside the room than outside.''

The man looked down and seemed shocked to find a weapon in his hand. ''Oh, I wouldn't worry about this,'' he said. With thick fingers he raised the lapel of his rumpled jacket and slipped the square-shouldered automatic into a brown leather holster. ''There now. Does that make you feel better?''

I nodded. ''It helps.'' It didn't help much.

Other than worrying over space on the arm rests, I hadn't paid much attention to the man on the plane. His face was soft, and there was a donut of soft flesh around his throat. His brown eyes were barely visible behind the glossy surface of his thick glasses, the nest of curly hair on his head had thinned enough to leave a shiny patch at the crown, and there was a good layer of whale blubber wrapped around his gut. At first glance, he seemed about as effective as a teddy bear with a thyroid problem.

But now that I was paying more attention, I could see that this man was fat more in the style of a Russian powerlifter than a couch potato. Under his Michelin Man exterior, there were plenty of steel belts. His shoulders bulked huge under his brown tweed coat and his arms were corded by more muscle than fat. Even without a gun I didn't doubt this man would have any trouble rendering me down to my component elements.

''I don't suppose you could tell me who you are?'' I asked.

''Of course,'' he replied pleasantly. Dimples appeared in his cheeks at the first hint of a smile. ''I'm Oswald Frazier.''

''Uh-huh.'' I tried to match his calm tone. The name went well with his harmless appearance—which immediately made me doubt that it was real. ''And do you make a habit of pointing a gun at people, Mr. Frazier?''

''I make a habit of being safe.'' He stepped further

into the room, turning slowly to survey the nearly empty scene. "It's a proclivity you might want to consider yourself, Ms. McKinnon."

A little headache started behind my eyes. I was beginning to wonder if there was anyone in Vermont who wasn't armed and who didn't know my name. "I'm glad to hear you take safety so seriously," I said. "Now would you mind telling me why you've been following me?"

"Only from necessity, I assure you," replied Frazier. "We've been looking for Michael Willmeyer for some time."

"And how did you—"

"Um," interrupted the fat man. He nodded toward the phone. "Do you need to finish your conversation?"

I had completely forgotten about the receiver still clenched in my fingers. Without taking my eyes off Frazier, I raised the handset to my ear. "Jen? You still there?"

"Ms. Skye!" she shouted. "I thought someone shot you."

It would have been funnier if the guy in front of me wasn't armed. "No," I said. "I'm fine. Thanks for the information."

"But what was that sound?" asked Jen. "Who were you talking to?"

"I'll get back to you," I said quickly. I could still hear Jen talking as I knelt, picked up the base of the phone, and returned the handset to its cradle.

The fat man smiled his mild smile. "You seem to have very able assistants."

"They're peachy," I agreed. "Now, I believe you

were explaining how you came to be snooping around after me?''

He nodded. ''As I said, I was trying to locate Willmeyer, not you.''

''I understand that part,'' I said. ''What you didn't tell me is how you knew I was going to meet Willmeyer.''

For the first time, a look of distress passed over Frazier's face. After a moment, he shrugged his heavy, rounded shoulders. ''I'm afraid there are some things I can't reveal at this time,'' he said. ''All I can say is that we had a very strong need to find Mr. Willmeyer. Otherwise, we would not have gone to such lengths.'' He walked across the room and looked down at the well-scrubbed patch in the middle of the floor. ''Is this where he died?''

''Yes.'' Taking advantage of the fat man's movement away from the door, I started edging toward the exit. ''It looks like someone beat you to it.''

He turned his round head toward me. ''Oh, we weren't going to kill Mr. Willmeyer. Far from it.''

''That's wonderful,'' I said, taking another step toward the door. ''Mind explaining just who 'we' would happen to be?''

Frazier turned away from me and looked toward the windows. ''Have you ever heard of the NSA?''

''National Security Agency?'' I nodded. ''I've heard of them. Mostly involved in code-breaking, things like that, right?''

He nodded without looking at me. ''Yes. Things like that.''

I reached the door and looked out. There was no one on the balcony and no one visible along the staircase or in the lobby below. If I wanted to make an escape, I certainly had my chance. Instead, I turned back to face Frazier. "So Count Yor . . . I mean, Willmeyer, really was an FBI agent?"

The fat man nodded again. "A good one."

"And Hoskins is . . ."

"Hoskins." Just saying the name, Frazier displayed more emotion than I had heard before—and it definitely was not fondness. He turned back to face me with as hard an expression as his round cheeks and padded chin could manage. "My advice is that you stay far away from Mr. Hoskins and his associates. Nothing that they say can be believed."

"But who is Hoskins?" I insisted. "If he's not with the FBI, then what's he doing here?"

The fat man didn't seem to be in a mood to answer this question. He turned abruptly and walked across to the windows. "Cowards," he muttered under his breath. "Filthy cowards." Despite the words, his voice was back to the smooth, calm tone he had used through most of our brief conversation.

"The people who shot Willmeyer?" I asked.

Frazier nodded. "They could have confronted him face-to-face. Instead they chose to end a man's life without even speaking to him." He turned my way. "I'd never commit such an act."

I started to say something else, then felt a sudden chill. If a little talk was what Frazier required before a kill, I might already be a candidate for his gun sights. "I need to be going," I said, fighting my own fear to speak slowly and evenly. "I have a story to research."

"Of course," Frazier said without apparent concern.

He flipped one of his big hands through the air. "Go ahead."

I turned with relief and took one step onto the balcony. But once again I froze. On the one hand, getting away from this demonstrably armed and possibly dangerous man seemed like a very sensible idea. On the other hand, if I stepped out of this room, I might never learn what had really gone on in there. Frazier, strange as he might be, was my only definite link with the forces that had killed my vampire.

I pivoted around and stepped back into the room. "Why are you here?" I asked.

Frazier raised one bushy eyebrow above the black plastic rim of his glasses. "I already told you. I was looking for Willmeyer."

"No," I said with a shake of my head. "You might have been looking for Willmeyer when you followed me to Williams Crossing, but you're not looking for him today." Demonstrating more confidence than I felt, I took a step toward him. "Willmeyer's been dead all day. Why are you here now?"

There was another moment of silence as the big man considered his answer. I had to give Frazier credit for one thing—he didn't speak without first engaging his brain. Unfortunately, from a reporter's point of view, that quality made him a very unlikely source of juicy information.

"You're right, of course," he said at last. "I knew of Willmeyer's death."

"So you came here to talk to me."

He nodded. "Yes." He raised one hand and rubbed at his round chin. The beard stubble on his face was stiff enough that I could hear the scratch of it against his hand from across the room. "I wanted to make contact with you—establish a relationship, you might say."

"And why did you want to do that?"

"Well . . ." He paused. By this time, Frazier's pauses were edging past mildly grating into the realm of extremely irritating. "You were in contact with Mr. Willmeyer for some time. It's possible that he may have passed along . . . information of a rather sensitive nature."

Suddenly my conversation with Frazier was starting to sound a lot like one of my talks with Hoskins. "Everything Willmeyer said to me is right there in my *Query* articles."

"Yes," Frazier agreed with a ponderous nod. "But there might have been other information—little details that failed to make the papers."

Now he was sounding a lot like Hoskins. I folded my arms across my chest and did my best to puzzle out the expression hiding behind those clunky glasses. "Just what is it you're hunting for? What did Willmeyer know that you find so interesting?"

I wasn't surprised when Frazier came back with no immediate answer. This time, I didn't give him time to think.

"You know," I said, "Hoskins asked me about what Willmeyer had said."

"Yes," Frazier agreed readily, "but you told him nothing."

I didn't know how the fat man had gathered this chunk of information, but what he said was true enough. Still, I didn't want Frazier to become too comfortable. "At first I was reluctant, but after we talked a bit," I said with a nod, "I knew I should share what I'd learned."

If I was looking for a reaction, I got one. Both of Frazier's bushy eyebrows jumped straight up and the muscles of his thick arms bunched so strongly that the seams of his jacket appeared to be in danger. "You shared information with that man?"

The tension in Frazier's voice was sharp enough that I found my own fear notching upward—but in for a penny, in for a pound. "Yep. We had quite a discussion on the subject."

"You didn't . . . I mean . . . he . . ." Frazier faded into silence, but this time he seemed more tongue-tied than contemplative. Up until this exchange, Frazier had seemed inhumanly composed, but the idea that I had passed along information to Hoskins left him so befuddled he was almost gasping for air.

Downstairs I heard the doors open and close, followed by the New England edge of Mrs. Grimes's voice. The fresh voices seemed only to add to the fat man's agitation. He looked toward the door, then the windows, then back to me. "We need to talk again, Ms. McKinnon. Soon."

I nodded slowly, fascinated to see actual sweat breaking out on Frazier's face. In less than five minutes, the man had gone from a figure of calm strength to a form visibly trembling with nerves. It would have been easier to enjoy his discomfort if I didn't clearly remember that the man was armed.

"I'm willing to talk," I said. "How do I reach you?"

Frazier's smile returned, but this time there was a disturbingly predaceous quality in those exposed choppers. "Don't worry," he said. "I'll find you." With that nonreassuring pronouncement, he stepped past me, squeezed through the narrow door, and disappeared around the curve of the balcony.

For the space of a dozen heartbeats, I couldn't move. I might have been paralyzed longer except for a new bout of coughing that started as a tickle, and ended with me bent almost double by a wracking round of explosive coughs. Along with the cough, I felt a flush of what seemed to be furnace heat against my skin. My flu definitely seemed to be getting worse.

There was a rapid thump of feet on the wooden stairs. "Miss McKinnon?" called Mrs. Grimes's voice from the balcony. "Are you all right?" Despite the problems I had caused, Mrs. Grimes still sounded genuinely concerned.

I nodded while I fought to recover my breath. "Yes," I replied, turning toward the innkeeper. "I'll be fine."

"You didn't sound—" started Mrs. Grimes. Then she stopped, and her mouth opened in a circle of surprise. "Oh, Miss McKinnon!"

I shook my head. "What? What's wrong?"

The innkeeper was literally trembling. She stumbled back a step and raised a shaky hand to cover her face. "Your face . . . you're . . ." That was as far as she got before she spun around and beat a hasty retreat down the stairs.

My feelings were dominated by puzzlement, but a big dose of fear was coming on fast. I could barely feel my feet as I crossed to my room, opened the door, and stepped over to the dresser. There was a tall, narrow mirror on the back of the heavy piece of furniture. The glass reflected a high bed heaped with quilts, a chest with a green serpentine top, and a shelf with an old brass lantern.

Shaking myself, I crept toward the glass and stepped fearfully in front of the dresser. Looking back at me from the glass was the white face of a vampire.

TWELVE

LOOKING AT MYSELF IN THE MIRROR HAD NEVER BEEN number one on my chart of Top 40 entertainment, but now it was on its way down—with a bullet.

I reached up and gingerly pressed the tips of my fingers against my cheeks and lips. The skin *felt* normal, and for a moment the pressure of my hands gave it a wash of color. But as soon as I took my fingers away, my cheeks paled to a color that made me look as if I had been living underground since birth. Even my lips had the faded look of a body recovered from beneath the ice of a frozen lake. My face wasn't quite the powder white of Yorga's, and I wasn't marked by the scars and blemishes that had disfigured my vampire interviewee. But I had no doubt that if I were to lay down on a table over at Armistead and Sons, someone would be reaching for an economy-sized jar of foundation.

When I had left the Stone River Inn that morning, I had noticed that I was looking a little illish, and Cooper had commented that I was looking pale. But what I saw in the mirror went beyond pale. In the space of a few hours, every trace of tan seemed to have vanished from my skin, leaving me with a complexion only cavefish could love.

I raised my hand again and noticed that I was shaking as badly as a politician in front of a grand jury. A burning cold knot of fear rolled up my spine and flickered in my skull.

"What's wrong with me?" I whispered hoarsely to the strange pale face in the glass. Part of the answer was blindingly obvious—whatever had turned FBI Agent Michael Willmeyer into tabloid throat-muncher Count Yorga was now percolating through my veins. Yet that told me nothing. Armistead had said that Yorga's affliction resembled a form of porphyria, but porphyria was a syndrome that could not be transmitted from person to person—not even by a bite.

A fresh cough started up my throat and I clamped a milky hand across my mouth. That was the magic moment when I put skin and cough together and realized that the increasing trouble in my throat and lungs was not a symptom of a returning flu, but only another aspect of this vampire malaise. Soon enough I could expect this experience to be enhanced by a sensitivity to sunlight, scars, and possibly death. Maybe even a fear of crosses and garlic.

I ran my trembling fingers across my face a final time and tried to control my beating heart. *Think,* I told myself. *Don't scream—engage your brain and figure a way out of this.* The trouble was, after thinking about it for a few seconds, screaming still seemed like my best option.

I heard muffled voices from downstairs and pulled my

attention away from the mirror. At any moment, I expected Mrs. Grimes to show up with the police, emergency med-techs, men in white coats—or all three. Letting myself be captured might be for the best, but I wasn't quite ready to take that chance. From what I had seen of the Williams Crossing Police Department, I might die of this disease while they were puzzling out what to do with me. I intended to keep my treatment in my own hands for as long as possible.

That was one decision out of the way. Next I only had to figure out what to do. If I had been near a city, my response might have been to run to the nearest doctor. But Williams Crossing didn't exactly look like the sort of place that was likely to have a doc-in-the-box on every corner. Getting medical attention on a snowy Sunday afternoon was probably going to be a little difficult. If I was going to find help, I was going to have to get out of the Stone River Inn and start looking.

My barely touched collection of vacation clothing was still inside the suitcase beside the bed. I dug through the contents and came up with a hooded snowsuit jacket padded by some ultra-thin ultra-insulating material intended to keep me warm without making me look like a blimp. I slipped it on, zipped it shut, and pulled the hood up around my head. The result didn't completely hide my bleached-out features, but at least it cast a shadow across my face. With this meager disguise in place, and my heart still doing a snare-drum imitation beneath my ribs, I headed out of the room and down the stairs.

As I reached the bottom step, I saw a couple dressed in Eddie Bauer's finest laughing with Mrs. Grimes near the front desk. I hung back and waited until the brief conversation ended and the pair took their all-natural fabrics out into the day, then hurried down the rest of the steps.

Mrs. Grimes turned toward me with a smile still on her face, but with one look at me the smile turned into an expression of shock. The lenses of her wire-frammed glasses seemed to amplify the growing fear in her eyes and she raised a flower-patterned dish towel to cover her face as I drew near. ''Stay back,'' she warned, her voice muffled by the cloth. ''Whatever you've got, I don't want it.''

''It's only the flu,'' I lied. ''I don't think I'm contagious.'' That last part might even be true. I was clear that I had come down with a bad case of white, but so far no one else appeared to be affected. If whatever Yorga had passed along to me could be spread through the air, we'd probably be in the midst of a vampire plague. My guess was that the ailment, whatever it was, required a more direct contact—like teeth planted in the forearm.

Mrs. Grimes gave a snort that made the towel flip out from her face like a curtain in a breeze. ''I'm not taking any chances,'' she said. ''I want you to collect your things and get out of here.''

My stay at the Stone River Inn had not exactly been filled with fond memories, but the idea of going out to find another room while looking like Casper's less-than-friendly sister wasn't too appealing. Nonetheless, I nodded. ''All right,'' I said. ''I need to run a few errands, but as soon as I get back, I'll get my things and check out.''

''Don't you bother to check out,'' said the innkeeper. ''Just grab your luggage and go. I'll mail you a bill.''

I stood for a moment, unsure whether I should ignore her for the present, or climb back up to retrieve all the clothing I had brought with me in hopes of impressing a man who didn't even make the trip. I felt woozy, dizzy, unable to make a decision. Part of it was probably the actual effects of the unknown illness, but a bigger part of the problem was just plain fear. I didn't know where to go, who to talk to, who to trust.

With options still tumbling through my head like laundry in a dryer, I turned toward the door and was almost outside before a question struck me. I turned back to Mrs. Grimes. "The man that came in here looking for me—did you talk to him?"

Mrs. Grimes lowered the towel long enough for me to see the frown tugging at her lips. "There was a man earlier." She held up a hand just above her head. "About this tall, gray hair."

It was interesting news, but not what I was after. "I'm talking about a guy that was bigger," I said. "Maybe six-four and at least three hundred pounds."

To my surprise, Mrs. Grimes suddenly smiled. "Oh, that's just Mr. Frazier," she exclaimed. "He came up yesterday. He's not looking for you." The way she said this made it obvious that Mrs. Grimes considered chasing after me to be an act that would be demeaning to any man.

"Is Mr. Frazier staying here?"

The innkeeper nodded. "He's up from Boston for the antiquing." She gave a wistful sigh. "Such a knowledgeable man when it comes to copper and wrought iron."

I wondered how Mrs. Grimes would feel if she knew about Frazier's familiarity with iron in the form of weaponry. In any case, the fat man's stay at the inn gave me an idea clear enough to part the sea of fear sloshing around my brain. Ignoring the way Mrs. Grimes cringed away from me as I moved, I walked over to the counter and picked up the registry.

"Leave that alone!" shouted the innkeeper from behind her cloth barrier. "I'll have to have it sanitized."

I pretended not to hear as I flipped through the pages to the most recent date. Sure enough, Frazier's name was written in the address block directly beneath mine in letters so neat they were nearly calligraphy. Below the name were a date and an address, each in the same flowing script. According to the registry, he had checked into the Stone River early on Saturday morning while I was enjoying the delightful company of the Williams Crossing police. If the registration was to be believed, he had made the drive to southern Vermont from 1952 Kennedy Lane in the Boston suburb of Newton. I ran my fingers over the dried blue ink and frowned. It was obvious that Frazier was some kind of spook, and it seemed highly unlikely that he would give his own home address, but there was something painfully familiar about the location spelled out on the page.

"Are you going to leave, or am I going to call the police?" said Mrs. Grimes. She edged closer, the dish towel pressed tightly to her face.

"I'm sure you're going to call the police anyway," I replied, "but I'm leaving."

Still trying to tickle a clue from my foggy memory, I walked out of the lobby and out onto the windswept porch. The crisp air brought on another hard cough, but the breeze also helped me calm down enough to think. I needed treatment. Whatever was wrong with me, it was obviously getting worse quickly. The white skin was just one problem. The coughing and other symptoms that I had written off as a resurgent flu bug might be signs of real damage from this new invader. If Armistead was even half right, and the disease did cause the same medical syndrome as porphyria, then I might only be in the foothills of a whole mountain range of suffering.

Finding Armistead seemed like a good first step. If nothing else, the mortician-in-training was familiar with Williams Crossing and the surrounding area. If there was a doctor to be found, he probably knew his or her location.

A group of children went past on the sidewalk as I climbed into my car. Self-consciously, I pulled the hood of the jacket down around my face and turned away, trying to hide the similarity between my skin and the snow. I glanced momentarily at my face in the rearview mirror, then forced myself to look at the road. All the way back to Armistead and Sons Funeral Parlor, I found myself alternating between periods of clarity and bouts of fear so sharp I nearly had to stop the car. By the time I slipped into the parking lot I was beginning to wonder if my smartest move wasn't to head straight to Boston and hope that someone there was clever enough to figure out what was wrong with me.

The funeral that had been getting started when Armistead led me out of the mortuary that morning had adjourned by the time I returned. Only a couple of cars were in the parking lot—including Cooper's shiny Mercedes. I pulled into the slot beside the SUV and climbed out of the car. Even with no one around, I kept my hands shoved deep into the pockets of the jacket and looked down at the ground as I walked to the door and stepped inside.

The place was empty. Despite the handful of cars outside, I could find no life in the visiting rooms, or in the chapel, or in the preparation room downstairs where two bodies still waited on tables for their turn on stage. I was just about to give up and leave when I heard a series of footsteps upstairs.

"Cooper?" I called. "Is that you?"

My only reply was another rapid series of steps and a solid thump, like a heavy door being slammed shut. A breeze rolled down the stairs and into the basement, ruffling the blue sheets that covered the two remaining bodies. For a moment, I had the eerie feeling that my embalmed roommates were going to sit up.

"Hello?" I said, or at least, tried to say. What came out of my clogged throat was more of a squeak than speech. The preparation room suddenly seemed very small, very warm, and very full of dead people. As frightened as I was by the disease bleaching all the color from my flesh like a reverse Ted Turner, I found I was still capable of an additional shiver.

I left the sheet-covered bodies to the basement and quickly climbed the stairs to the ground floor. Despite the noises I had heard, I still saw no sign of any feet to go along with the footsteps.

"Cooper?" I called in a voice too soft to be heard more than ten feet away. "Are you there?"

There was a shuffling, dragging sound, and a creak of hinges at my back. I spun around and found myself facing an empty hallway. "Cooper?" I tried again, risking a little more volume.

If I hadn't already scaled the heights of nervous, I

might have run straight for the door. But when you're standing on an Everest worth of fear, all directions are down. With my legs trembling and a colony of ants walking along my spine, I advanced down the long hallway and stepped into the coffin showroom.

The selection of gleaming metal and polished wood had a sort of grisly dignity about it. I glanced quickly at the top of the line model, but it was one of the midrange oblong boxes that caught my attention. In the corner of the room was a round-cornered bronze coffin edged in bright steel trim. In a collection of twenty thousand-dollar boxes, there was nothing particularly exceptional about this one—except that it was closed. All of the other sarcophagi were open on at least one end—the better to display their linings of glistening purple satin and soft blue velvet. And I was quite certain that on my previous visit to the room, all the boxes had been open.

For a good ten seconds, I stood and stared at the closed lid with my breath and heartbeat combining to reach a jet engine roar in my ears. Then, before I could lose what little nerve still remained to me, I hurried across the floor, grabbed a handle, and flipped up the lid.

Agent Hoskins lay on his side, surrounded by shiny peach fabric that was splashed with very unartistic streaks of reddish-brown. There was an opening in his skull just above his left eye. It was a neat, clean circle as nice and round as could be hoped for, but I was quite certain that people shouldn't have circular holes in their skulls. Not even neat ones. From the glazed, fixed stare of his bloodshot eyes, I suspected that Agent Hoskins wasn't going to be offering an opinion.

It was about this point that my legs decided that my brain was making some very poor choices. Without further advice from above, they spun me around and started me toward the door.

But the door was already occupied. By a vampire.

A woman with long, classic features and chilly blue eyes stood just inside the entrance to the mortuary. She wore a unbuttoned tan trench coat that gaped open to reveal a dark sweater and snug jeans around a trim figure. She was tall and thin, with long legs and cheekbones high enough to land her on a magazine cover. Her skin was a milky perfection so untainted with color that she might have been carved from alabaster, or painted over in Sear's Best Weatherbeater. Only her hair—snowy white at the roots, but darkening to brown at the ends—kept her from epitomizing the monochromatic ideal.

''I didn't do it,'' said the female vampire.

It took me a moment to realize what crime she was denying. I glanced around at Hoskins's body, then looked quickly back to the vampire. Only on this second glance did I notice the dark, snub-nosed revolver in her hand. My feeling that everyone in the charming little village of Williams Crossing was carrying a weapon—everyone but me—seemed to be confirmed.

''Who . . .'' I started, but my voice caught in my throat. I took as deep a breath as I could manage and tried again. ''Who are you?''

''It appears that I'm someone with the same problem you have,'' she replied. Her blue eyes darted from side to side, and she craned her neck to scan the gloomy parking lot quickly before turning back my way. ''I'm looking for Michael.''

''Michael?''

She nodded and took a step toward me. ''Michael Willmeyer.''

''Oh,'' I said. ''Count . . . I mean, yes.'' I swallowed a harp lump of fear and hoped for the best. ''Mr. Willmeyer's dead.''

The woman frowned, but the news didn't seem to come as a terrible shock. ''Damn,'' she snapped. ''I thought he might be.'' She waved the barrel of the gun my way. ''Do you know who did it?''

''No,'' I said. ''Not really.'' I looked at the gun and licked my dry lips. ''I know I didn't do it.''

The vampire nodded. ''I didn't think so.'' With a deft flick of her thumb, she lowered the hammer on the revolver then slipped both hand and gun into the pocket of her coat. ''Michael came here to meet you. That much information I was able to gather on my own. Then what?''

''He was killed,'' I said. ''At least I think he was killed.'' I pointed a shaky finger toward the body in the coffin. ''The local coroner said it was a heart attack, but the FBI sent this man to investigate the death, and now he's dead, too.''

''Batkowitcz?'' The woman shook her head sharply, sending a curtain of white-to-dark hair whipping around her face. ''He was no FBI agent.''

''Who's Batkowitcz?'' I asked.

The woman nodded toward the coffin. ''He is. Your dead man.''

I looked at Hoskins's lifeless form and bit my lip. ''But he told me—''

''Whatever he told you was a lie,'' she said. With a heavy sigh, she walked over to the coffin and stood looking down at the dead man inside. "All any of them ever knew how to do was lie, Michael included."

I didn't know what was going on, but I knew it was time to start over. "Who are you?" I tried again. "Did you know Mr. Willmeyer?"

The woman nodded. "I used to think so." She reached up, grabbed the edge of the coffin and lowered it gently, hiding Hoskins's body. "Until Michael was forced into hiding, we had been partners for almost two years."

By now, some of the fog of fear had started to break up, but the mist of confusion was still plenty thick. I had so many questions for this woman, I couldn't decide which to ask first. "Why did he . . . I mean . . . how . . ." I stopped and shook my head. "Who do you work for?"

The woman gave this a silent consideration that reminded me of Oswald Frazier's maddening cogitation. She stood looking at me with her blue eyes unblinking and her white lips pressed tightly together. "You've heard of the Secret Service," she said at last.

"Sure," I said.

"Well, we're not them," said the woman. She looked away from me a moment, surveying the door and hallway. "But we have a similar task—to safeguard the nation. Watch over certain people. Protect the keys."

"Keys?" I said. "What keys?"

"The keys to some very important information," she replied, "and some very dangerous weapons." She raised up on the balls of her feet and peered away into the shadowed interior of the mortuary.

I took advantage of the woman's distraction to begin moving toward the door. As interesting as her story was,

I wanted to have a shot at freedom should she decide to stop using words and start using bullets. But I wasn't going anywhere until I asked the most important question. "What happened to Willmeyer?" I said. "And to you? And to me? What's wrong with us?"

The woman looked down at her own pale hands and flexed her white, unmarked fingers. "You're a reporter, right?"

The nonsequitur baffled me, but I nodded. "Right."

"Have you ever reported on a bank robbery?"

"It's been a while, but yeah. I have. Why do you ask?"

"If you've been around a bank robbery, then you've probably seen the dye cartridges that banks plant in their money." The woman snapped her fingers. "The cartridge goes off, and both the money and the robber are covered in dye."

"I've seen that happen," I agreed. "What I don't see is what this has to do with what's going on here."

"I'm getting to that," said the woman with an impatient tone. "This disease is like those dye cartridges. It's not really intended to kill you, just . . . mark you until you can be found."

"Found by who?" I asked.

"By the people that made it." She waved toward the dead agent in his half-open coffin. "By Batkowitcz and his cronies."

"Made?" It took me a moment to make sense of the word. Diseases were things that you caught, but nobody made them, they just were. At least, that was the way it was supposed to be. "Are you telling me that this thing came from some kind of germ-warfare lab?'' Suddenly my white skin felt as cold as it looked.

''Not exactly,'' said the woman. ''Look, I don't have time for this. It's your turn to talk.''

''Me?'' I shook my head. ''But I don't know anything.''

The vampire rolled her blue eyes. ''I can believe that easily enough,'' she said. Suddenly she pulled the pistol from her pocket and jammed it straight at me. ''But for starters, how about telling me how you got infected with AV?''

''AV?'' Learning the name—or at least the initials—of the infection was a nice piece of data, but when I was looking into the business end of a squat, ugly pistol, it didn't seem as interesting as it might be in other circumstances.

The vampire raised her weapon until the black opening of the revolver was leveled at my eyes. ''Just tell me what happened so I can—''

Her words were interrupted by a dry, flat crack that came from behind me. I looked around and saw a small hole in the calm blue-and-green patterned wallpaper that was surrounded by a thinning cloud of plaster dust. A second hole suddenly appeared with another crack. I looked back toward the woman, and was surprised to see her lying flat on the ground.

''What are you doing?'' I asked.

''Idiot!'' she hissed back. ''Don't you know when someone is shooting at you?''

My legs, which had been interrupted in their earlier attempt to carry my worthless brain to safety, seized on this opportunity. I spun around and flew out the door into the parking lot just as wood chips showered from the door frame. My feet slipped on the snow, but I managed to stay upright as I dived among the scattered cars. From behind me, I heard the hard, deep cough of a pistol firing twice, then twice more in close succession. I didn't turn to look.

The sun was sinking behind a fresh wall of gray clouds, and the slush on the parking lot was fast freezing into a skating rink of lumpy black ice. I slipped, bounced off the fender of a snow-frosted hearse, spun in a 360-degree one-footed spin that would have impressed Dorothy Hamill, and kept right on running. Once I was off the parking lot, I made better progress in the loose snow. Only after I had gone another hundred yards and stumbled into the street did I remember that the only vehicle I had was back at the mortuary.

It took another ten steps before this information made it to my feet and halted my headlong panic. I skidded to a stop; hurried to the side of the road; pressed my body up against the shaggy, damp bark of a maple tree; and peered back into the direction I had just come. Shadows moved inside the open door of the mortuary. Neither the female vampire or the unseen flinger of bullets made an appearance.

A sudden sharp gust of icy wind blew along the street, cutting through my oh-so-colorful-and-thin ski jacket like a Mack truck hitting a Yugo. A fresh supply of snowflakes began to tumble from the darkening sky. Suddenly the quaint little town of neat shops and well-tended churches seemed as cold and hostile as the middle of Antarctica. I shivered, and risked sticking my head a little further away from the tree. My rental car was sitting at the edge of the parking lot, just where I had left it. The vehicle was no more than a hundred yards away, right out in the open and ready to go. But walking back to my car seemed about as sensible as making meatballs in a shark pond.

I looked in the other direction. No more than fifty yards down the street was an antique shop where depression glass and obscure wood-working tools sat shoulder to shoulder in well-lit windows. Inside there was bound to be warmth and a phone. But my legs, which had been so anxious to escape the mortuary, now seemed content to quiver behind the maple tree.

I risked another glance at the mortuary and saw that there was one vehicle missing from the small array that had been in the parking lot when I had arrived. Cooper Armistead's ridiculously expensive SUV was gone. The first thing I felt was frustration—somehow Cooper and I had managed to miss each other within the hallways and chapels of the mortuary. Close on the heels of that feeling was a rush of relief—at least Cooper had made it out of there before the gunslingers showed up to put holes in FBI agents and dull wallpaper.

Somewhere in the near-distance a siren began to wail. As the sound grew louder, a pair of figures ran from the side of the mortuary and disappeared around the back. I couldn't tell much about either of them, but from their bulk and nonreflective nature, I didn't think either of the escapees was my female vampire. A few minutes later red-and-blue lights strobed along the street as a pale-blue sedan turned onto the road and rolled in my direction.

Despite the flashing lights and blaring noise, the police car moved along the road at a pace more appropriate to a parade than an emergency. With a final glance toward Armistead and Sons, I managed to tear myself away from the protective mass of the maple tree and stagger out into the center of the road. I waved my arms overhead and held my ground as the blue sedan slowly closed the distance.

The way things had been going since I arrived in Williams Crossing, I wouldn't have been surprised if the car had tried to run me down, but the vehicle came to a halt a good twenty feet away. It sat there idle in the middle of the road, lights and siren still going. I hurried up to the driver's side and found myself looking through a closed window at the drawn gray face of Sheriff Loudermilk.

"It's an emergency," I said, shouting to be heard above the siren. "Agent Hoskins is dead."

I couldn't tell whether he could hear me, but after a moment the siren ended its whoop and the window began to open with a soft whine of electric motors. The sheriff's eyes surveyed me. "You look like you saw a ghost, Ms. McKinnon. Fact, you look like you're the next thing to a spook yourself."

"Close enough," I said with a nod. "There's someone—"

Loudermilk cut me off with a wave of his bony hand. "Can't talk now," he said. "There's a report of someone discharging a weapon over at Armistead and Sons."

"I know. I was there."

The sheriff scowled at me. "Wasn't you that was firing a gun, was it?"

I shook my head. "There was a woman, and Agent Hoskins is dead, and—"

"Hold on there." For the first time, Sheriff Loudermilk actually looked stunned. "You say Hoskins is dead?"

I started to nod, but the motion quickly turned into a tremor that shook me head to toe. "I saw him laid out in a coffin."

"That doesn't mean—"

"There was a hole in his head."

Loudermilk winced. "That's not generally the kind of thing you want to see."

"You need to get someone." I raised my head and looked over the car toward the silent bulk of the mortuary. "Call the state police. Or call the FBI. Call someone."

This suggestion didn't go over well with the sheriff. "You hold on right there," he said. "I already let one federal agent walk in here; I'm not about to get started with more." He looked toward the funeral parlor. "This town is in my charge, and I mean to settle this matter myself."

"You don't understand," I said, still looking through the screen of trees at the side of the road. "Something's going on here. Something big."

Loudermilk snorted. "I understand one thing. If there's laws to be enforced in Williams Crossing, then I'm the one to—"

It was at that point in his speech that the passenger-side window of the squad car exploded inward. Sheriff Loudermilk's mouth hung open for a second, then closed with a clack. His hands slipped from the steering wheel, and he slumped down in his seat.

I stepped back from the car just as another bullet angled off the roof with a sound like a hammer striking an anvil. That was definitely my signal to depart. I turned and ran away into the gathering night.

THIRTEEN

ADRENALINE IS A WONDERFUL THING—UNTIL IT RUNS out. By the time my exhaustion overcame my fear, I was blocks away from the mortuary. I was also thoroughly lost.

I cut a path through knee-deep drifts and slowed to a stop under an ornate street light. My breath steamed and curled amid the slow-falling flakes of snow. The cold air seared my lungs and my legs felt like overcooked spaghetti. If anyone had started shooting at that moment, I would have had to throw up my hands and surrender.

Standing in the cold street, lost between neat houses and quaint stores, I watched snow gradually filling in the few bare patches of asphalt and wondered what to do next. Loudermilk was dead. Hoskins was dead. The female vampire might also be dead. Even if she wasn't, I wasn't sure it was too smart to look for someone who had been so eager to point a gun my way. I supposed that Deputy Doug was an option—he might be incompetent, but he should be able to operate a telephone long enough to call in the marines. In any case, there seemed to be no other option for me but to get out of Williams Crossing and do it quickly.

I forced my tired legs into a slow walk and trudged around the corner in hopes of finding a bus stop, train station, or taxi that could deliver me back to places where no one was shooting—or at least, where they weren't shooting at me. Cab fare from Williams Crossing back to Boston would probably take a month of my pay, and the idea of getting Mr. Genovese to pay for it was more laughable than a dozen *Query* headlines, but that seemed like a minor consideration at the moment.

Suddenly the light from the street lamp seemed to triple in intensity. I stood there on the corner, blinking against the abrupt increase in glare. With a hand pressed to my face, I tilted my head back and peered up between my fingers.

It wasn't the lamp.

The brilliant glow was coming from somewhere higher, from somewhere in the gray depths of the snow-laden clouds. Shifting pearlescent light rained down, so bright and hot that snowflakes melted in its path. A warm rain pattered against my coat and splashed in my face. For the space of a heartbeat the light shone down on me as if I was the centerpiece in some demented Christmas pagent. Then, just as quickly as it had begun, the light snapped off.

''Great!'' I shouted up at the sky. ''That's just great. And who are you guys with? The CIA?'' Whoever, or whatever it was, the road-hog UFO did not deign to reply.

With my eyes still dazzled from the light, I turned my

attention back to the snow-covered ground and started walking. The first block of stores I passed were all decorated with signs informing me that they had closed. So was the next. Huddling in my jacket, which was more decorative than effective, I began to wonder if I would freeze before someone managed to shoot me. I moved as quickly as I could past an empty park where snow hung heavy on the thick branches of spruce trees, then around a tall, stone church, and found myself looking at a very familiar sight. Just across the street, the Stone River Inn loomed over the dark street. Inviting yellow light shown from its windows and spilled out onto its porch.

For a minute, I only stood there and stared. I had left the inn with Mrs. Grimes threatening to have the police throw me out. For anyone hunting me in Williams Crossing, the Stone River would be an obvious place to pin me down. But it was also the place where I had left my luggage, my notes, and much of my cash. If I was going to get out of town, I needed to make one last call on Mrs. Grimes.

A pair of cars moved slowly along the street outside the inn. I waited until the lights had faded into the distance, then dashed across the slushy street, up the steps, and across the salt-crusted porch to the front door. I raised my face to the small window at the top of the door and peered inside. My view was blocked by frost, and what little of the pane was uncovered quickly became fogged by my breath, but the slice of lobby in my view seemed to be clear. I opened the door as quietly as I could and slipped inside.

The lobby was deliciously warm. Snowflakes melted off the nylon hood of my jacket and dripped down my cheeks. I tiptoed across the hardwood floor and was on the fourth step up to my room before I heard the door open at my back. I whirled around, expecting to see Oswald Frazier, or the female vamp, or some other person with a strong interest in the Second Amendment right to bear arms. Instead, I found Cooper Armistead looking up at me from the doorway.

"Savvy!" Cooper called. He closed his eyes for a moment and let out a deep breath. "Thank God."

I went back down the steps. "There were people at your father's place."

He nodded. "I know. I was afraid they might have taken you—or worse."

"I'm fine." In fact, I felt like every joint in my body was on its way to becoming liquid, but I didn't want Cooper to see how nervous I really was. "I'm fine," I repeated, "but Sheriff Loudermilk is—"

"I know," Cooper interrupted. He reached out and took my hand. "Savvy, these people . . . I don't think there's anything they wouldn't do to get the information they want."

"We need to get out of here," I said with all the urgency I could muster. I had no doubt that Cooper was marked along with me. Both of us needed to put Williams Crossing in the rearview ASAP. "Let me grab my things, then we have to go."

Cooper nodded. "All right," he said.

I pulled my hand free from his and started for the stairs. I only mounted the first steps before a voice called me back. This time I was interrupted by the appearance of Mrs. Grimes.

She emerged from the dining room with a scowl on

her face. ''So you did come back,'' Mrs. Grimes said in an angry tone.

I nodded. ''Don't worry. I'm not staying long. As soon as I get my things, I'll be out of here.''

''Good,'' said the innkeeper. ''That man was here looking for you again. I told him you were leaving.''

Wonderful. Not only was I being pursued by killers, Mrs. Grimes was handing them my itinerary. ''You have my address,'' I said. ''Send me a bill for the room.''

The innkeeper gave her loudest snort yet. ''Don't you worry about that. I'll be sending you a bill for the room, and the cleaning, and all that missing furniture. That trashy paper of yours will have to pay for it all.''

It was clear that Mrs. Grimes had never met Bill Genovese or his staff of tightwad accountants. I didn't bother to reply, but marched up the stairs to my room.

I got there only to find that someone had already paid me a visit. In my brief and erratic stay at the Stone River Inn, I had barely had a chance to unpack my wardrobe. But someone else had seen to it—my clothing was scattered from one end of the place to the other. The pages of my notebook had been ripped from their binding and scattered around the room like ticker tape after a parade. My tape recorder was nowhere in sight. And it wasn't only my things that had suffered an attack. The paintings had been pulled down from the walls. Chairs were overturned. Even the mattress had been sliced open, leaving a mound of loose feathers heaped in the center of the room.

''Great,'' I muttered. I slammed the door, causing a small tornado of feathers to circle the room. ''I'll just bet that Mrs. Grimes adds this to my bill.''

There was a distant, tingly feeling in my hands and

feet that I recognized as the beginnings of shock. Here I was in a town where half the people I knew were dead and the other half were trying to kill me. Mysterious lights were hovering in the sky and FBI agents were lying dead. Add to that a disease boiling through my body that had been cooked up in some germ-warfare lab, and you had a good start on a major breakdown. Toss on a dose of solid exhaustion. Knowing that someone had been pawing through my underwear was just the cherry on top of the impending-mental-collapse parfait.

The door opened at my back. I didn't even bother to look. "Savvy?" said Cooper. "Do you need some . . ." He stepped up beside me and his voice trailed away as he saw the interior of the room. "Wow. Someone really worked this place over."

"Uh-huh," I agreed.

"Do you want me to help you get your things?"

"Uh-huh."

Cooper turned toward me. "Savvy? Are you all right?"

"Oh, sure. I'm fine." I staggered forward a step and picked up a page from my torn notebook. My fingers felt stiff and wooden. "I'm fine."

"I don't think you are." Cooper walked around in front of me. Gently, he pulled the paper from my fingers and gripped both my hands in his. "Savvy, you have to let me help you."

"Just . . . just get me out of here." I hadn't coughed in hours, but a fresh bout seized me at that moment. I coughed so explosively that only Cooper's grip kept me from tumbling to the floor.

"I have to get you to a doctor," he said.

I nodded weakly. "Do you think they'll know what

to do?'' I asked when I got my breath back.

''I'm sure they will.'' Cooper leaned down, his handsome face only inches from mine, concern stamped across his clean features. ''But if you really want me to help you, you have to tell me what it is everyone is after.''

I frowned. ''What?''

''All these people that are chasing you.'' He tossed his head in a gesture that took in the whole town. ''They all want something from you. Some piece of information.''

''But I don't . . . I don't know anything.''

Cooper's frowned. ''What about that man? The one you called Yorga? Didn't he tell you something?''

''No.''

''There must be something,'' he insisted. ''All these people couldn't be dying for nothing.''

''I don't know anything,'' I replied sharply. ''Willmeyer did bring me here to listen to his story, but he was killed before we got started.''

''Really?'' The mortician-in-training raised one dark eyebrow. ''But I thought you passed some information along to Agent Hoskins.''

I shook my head. ''That was a lie. I only said that because I wanted to see if . . . if . . .'' I stopped and looked at Cooper in confusion. ''How did you know about that? I never told you about saying anything to Hoskins.''

Cooper's grip on my hands sudden grew from comforting to painful. ''Are you telling me that you didn't say anything to Hoskins?''

I tried to pull away, but Cooper's hands were clamped

tight. "You're in this," I said as realization sank in. "You're one of them."

He laughed. It was a hard, mean sound. "You don't even know what you're talking about."

I gave a sudden jerk and managed to loosen myself from his grip. I looked into his blue, blue eyes and felt a rising tide of anger. Stupid. I had been really, really stupid. "I may not know everything that's going on," I said, "but I know a rat when I see one."

"Ooh," he said, his voice filled with mock injury. "I think someone feels a bit betrayed." He laughed and brushed a curl of dark hair away from his forehead. "You didn't really think I was hanging around you because you're so beautiful, did you?" He sneered. "I'm afraid I like my women with a healthier skin tone."

I took a step back from him and gave the room a quick scan. An antique bed warmer with a dark iron pan and a handle of polished hickory leaned against the wall near the windows. It looked old, and heavy, and just right for smashing the skull of a smug bastard.

I looked at Cooper and did my best to return his smile. "Which ones?" I asked, taking a slow step toward the bed warmer.

Cooper looked at me with supreme scorn. "What's that?"

I took another step. "Which ones do you work for?"

"That's easily answered," he replied. Cooper turned his face toward the door and raised his voice a notch. "You may as well come on in. She knows nothing."

The door popped open and Oswald Frazier squeezed through the frame. "I always suspected as much," he said.

I looked back and forth between them. There was a

sick, acid taste in the back of my throat. Sometimes you're just paranoid; sometimes everyone really is out to get you. "I know this trick."

The fat man pursed his full lips in a puzzled expression. "Trick?"

I nodded. "You two were playing good cop bad cop." I jerked my thumb toward Cooper. "His job was to butter me up, make me feel like he was close to me. Then you come in and act like Darth Vader."

"Please," said Oswald. He eased the door closed and leaned his bulk against the wooden panel. "My behavior was completely proper. I never threatened you."

"No," I agreed. "You just let me see your gun and hinted that you were going to kill me."

Frazier waggled a thick finger in my direction. "You shouldn't have pretended to know more than you did, Ms. McKinnon. Telling me that you had passed information to Hoskins caused us all a lot of trouble."

"It kept me alive," I said. I reached down with what I hoped was a casual gesture and closed my fingers around the handle of the bed warmer, then I turned my attention to Cooper. "How did you do it?" I asked. "How did you fool the sheriff and the rest of them? They all seemed to know you."

Cooper folded his arms over his broad chest. "They do know me. I grew up here, my father really does own the mortuary, and I really am home from school." He glanced over at Frazier. "Just not the kind of school people around here might think."

"But how—" I started.

Frazier waved a heavy hand through the air. "Enough," he said. "Move away from the window, Ms. McKinnon."

"Why?" I lifted the bed warmer slightly from the floor and felt its heft. "So you won't break the glass?"

The first honest smile I had seen appeared on the fat man's lips. "Exactly." He raised his gun. "Now, move."

Almost all my life, people had been overlooking me. I was the shortest kid in my class. The girl in the back row. No one ever expected much from me. Most of the time, it was simply frustrating, but every now and then, it pays to be underrated. Following orders, I took a single step away from the window. Then I turned toward Cooper and swung the bed warmer with a two-handed backhand like Chris Evert going for a shot down the line.

The metal pan was halfway to his nose before the smile suddenly fell from the fake mortician's face. That was all the reaction he had time for. The black iron struck Cooper on the shoulder, bounced off, and caught him in the jaw—not quite as clean a blow as I had hoped for, but enough to send him spinning back. He stopped, stood trembling for a moment, and fell limp to the floor.

With one bad guy neatly dispatched, I raised my trusty bed warmer and turned to take on number two.

And then a gun was pressed against my forehead.

In the grip of Frazier's big hand, the pistol looked like a child's toy, but the opening that was hard against my skin felt as large as the mouth of a cannon. "I'd advise you to stop, Ms. McKinnon," he said with chilling calm.

The bed warmer slipped from my numb fingers and fell to the floor with a heavy thud. "I'm stopped," I said.

Frazier nodded. "Good." He pulled the gun away from my forehead and another smile touched his plump lips. "Shooting you from that close would have made a terrible mess."

I nodded, but I was no longer looking at him. Instead, I was watching as the door to the room slowly crept open. "Who was he?" I asked, stalling for time.

The fat man shook his head. "Who are you talking about?"

"Count Yorga," I said. "Michael Willmeyer. Who was he?"

Frazier shrugged his large, rounded shoulders. "Just someone who got in over his head," said the big man. "Someone not unlike yourself."

In the center of the room, Cooper Armistead started to get to his knees, then slumped back to the floor. A milky white figure moved silently into the room, stepped over his body, and advanced on the fat man.

"But what about—" I started.

"Quiet," said Frazier. He directed his gun at the center of my chest. "No more games, Ms. McKinnon. No more answers. Say good-bye."

There was a solid, unmistakable click as the woman cocked the hammer of her black revolver. "I like the sound of that, Oswald," she said. "Have you said your own prayers? Are you ready to go?" The fat man started to turn, but the woman jammed her gun hard into his padded back. "Don't even try," she said firmly. "Drop it. Now."

The pistol fell from Frazier's hands and clattered across the hardwood floor. "Ms. Roenton. How nice to see you."

"I'm sure," the woman replied. She tilted her head, letting her bicolor hair fall to one side as she looked up at the big man's face. "Is that what you said to Michael before you shot him?"

"I never—"

The woman jammed the gun in harder, pushing until the first joint of her fingers was lost in the roll around Frazier's midsection. "Tell me the truth. What did you use?"

He shook his head. "We never—"

"What did you use on Michael!" she screamed. "Tell me, you fat son of a bitch, or I'll put you on a .38 caliber diet!"

"Nicotine," Frazier replied softly.

The answer puzzled me. "You killed him with cigarettes?"

"With nicotine," said the fat man. He twisted his head back and glanced toward the female vampire. "We had hoped to bring Mr. Willmeyer in alive, but it seems that that infection he carried gives its victims a certain extra sensitivity to such stimulants."

The vampire only stared at him. Her white arms fairly vibrated with tension, and I tensely waited for the sound of her gunshot. But it didn't come.

"Excuse me," I said, hoping that my voice wouldn't push the woman over the edge. "But what now? What are we going to do?"

The vampire shifted her blue eyes toward me. "We?"

I winced. "I mean . . . well . . . we are both infected with this disease. Maybe if we work together we could find the cure." I paused and swallowed hard. "If there is a cure."

Frazier cleared his throat. "It so happens that there is a cure. If you're interested in finding it, why not let me take you to those who know how to help. Just put down your weapon, and—''

''No thanks,'' the woman said quickly. ''Considering how your people treated Michael, I don't think I want you sticking a needle in my arm.''

''We can be reasonable, Ms. Roenton,'' the fat man promised. ''Drop your weapon and we'll make a deal.''

The woman gave a bark of hard laughter. ''If I drop my weapon, the only deal we'll make will be how fast I die.''

Cooper Armistead moaned on the floor. He put his shaking hands flat against the polished oak and started to push himself up. Without ever letting Frazier escape the sights of her weapon, the woman walked over and delivered a perfectly casual, perfectly viscous kick to Cooper's arm, toppling him over on his side. The spy-in-training screamed like a baby.

The woman smiled. ''You know,'' she said, ''that was very satisfying.'' She glanced down at the black pistol in her hand, and then up at Frazier. ''Maybe I should shoot you, just for the fun of it.''

''Excuse me,'' I said again. Nervousness made my breath come out in halting gasps. I had to stop and pull in several jerky breaths before I could manage another sentence. ''If Mr. Frazier knows where to find the cure, maybe we shouldn't shoot him.''

The woman scowled. ''We. We. We. I still don't know why I should trust you any more than I do these lying sacks. You were the one in the room when Michael died.''

''Count Yorga—I mean, Michael—came here to see me,'' I said. ''He didn't consider me an enemy.''

The woman frowned, but this time it seemed more

out of puzzlement than anger. "I never understood why Michael would want to talk to you."

"Neither do I," I said. That wasn't completely true—several murky ideas were swimming around at the back of my brain—but none of them was ready to face the light of day.

For a moment, the whole room seemed to be frozen in place. Frazier stood with his thick hands out to his sides. Cooper lay facedown on the floor in a growing puddle of drool. The woman stood with her gun clutched tightly in her long, white fingers. I waited tensely for something to break—and hoped it wouldn't be me.

"Tie them up," the woman said suddenly into the silence.

"What?" I asked.

She nodded toward the two men. "You want to prove you're worth something to me? Tie these two up so we can get out of here."

I felt a tremendous relief. Tying the men up sounded like there wasn't going to be any more shooting. It wasn't as if I had any affection for these two—I certainly didn't mind seeing Cooper suffering a little pain and embarrassment—but I had already seen my quota of dead people for one vacation weekend. "What should I tie them with?" I asked.

The vampire rolled her eyes. "Be creative," she said.

I got creative. Ropework was not my strong suit—if there was knot-tying in the Girl Scouts, I never got that far—but I went with the theory that if you tied *enough* knots, one of them was bound to hold. Two lamp cords, a curtain pull, and a pair of my best silk pajama bottoms later, the two men were tied as tightly as I was going to get them. Cooper had lain unconscious while I lashed his hands and feet behind his back. Oswald Frazier had taken a seat in a Shaker chair and waited patiently while I fumbled to run the cords that bound his arms and legs to the chair. In fact, he had cooperated so easily that I suspected he could snap the thin cords around his thick wrists with a barely a twitch.

"Now what?" I asked as I pulled tight the last in a long line of knots.

The vampire quickly surveyed my work. She nodded what I took as approval, but she didn't put away her gun. "Now we leave." She walked a step closer to Frazier and stood looking down at him with an expression I couldn't read. "Remember this," she said. "It would have been easier to kill you."

The fat man nodded. "Yes," he replied, his voice as calm as ever. "And a good deal safer."

The vampire only looked at him for a moment, then spun on her bootheels and headed for the door. I hurried to follow her.

There was no sign of Mrs. Grimes or other guests on the balcony, or in the lobby below. I felt like a player in some elaborate caper film as we moved silently down the stairs and headed for the front door. The vampire had her hand on the knob when she suddenly paused.

"What is it?" I asked.

"Listen."

I listened. At first I heard nothing but wind and the soft patter of snow against the sides of the old frame building, but gradually a sound rose in the background. Police sirens. This time, it didn't seem to be the music of a lone lawmaker, but a whole chorus of cops on their way. "Sounds like someone discovered Sheriff Loudermilk," I said.

The vampire let out a breath that whistled through her teeth. "We need to get moving," she said. "When we get to your vehicle, start the engine, but leave the lights off until we're out on the highway."

I winced. "Umm, okay, but I'm afraid my car's not *right* outside."

"Where is it?"

"A mile or so away. Back at the mortuary."

"The mortuary right beside where the sheriff was killed."

"That's the one."

"Which is probably where all those police are headed."

I nodded.

The woman pocketed her gun and put her face in her hands. For the moment she looked tired, gaunt, and not at all well. "You can bet that stupid deputy is going to point them here next. We're going to have to locate some wheels and get out of here before—"

Whatever she was planning, her words were interrupted as the front door of the Stone River Inn suddenly opened. I felt sluggish, almost frozen, and the woman stepped back and pressed herself into a space behind the tall grandfather clock. A dark form moved from the snowy porch into the lobby. The vampire's white hand darted into her coat pocket and produced the black snub-nosed revolver. The newcomer stepped through the doorway. I caught a glimpse of broad shoulders and a leather jacket, and corduroy pants and a face topped with dark hair running to gray.

The vampire thumbed back the hammer on the pistol. Her finger slipped inside the trigger guard.

"Wait!" I shouted. The paralysis suddenly left me

and I jumped forward. ‘‘Don’t shoot him.’’

Standing in the doorway, Jimmy Knowles blinked against the light. He looked down at me, and I saw a flash of happiness that was quickly replaced by concern. ‘‘Savvy?’’

‘‘Yes.’’

He reached out and touched my face with the back of his hand. ‘‘You look terrible.’’

I took his hand in mine and squeezed it hard. ‘‘Flatterer.’’

FOURTEEN

"WOULD YOU MIND TELLING ME WHAT YOU ARE DOING here?" I demanded.

Jimmy squinted at the road ahead. "At the moment, I'm trying to drive a big car on a narrow, icy road in a snowstorm without using my headlights."

"That's not what I meant."

"I know," he said. "But before I start telling you about my weekend drive, I thought maybe you could tell me why we're running from the police?"

"We're not actually running," I said carefully. "We just don't have time to talk to them now."

"Right," said Jimmy. "And when will we talk to them?"

I looked around at the surrounding streets and made sure that there were no other cars in sight. "Hopefully never."

Since leaving the Stone River Inn, we had been creeping along the side roads of Williams Crossing. With only the occasional glow from the moon shining through gaps in the clouds to light our way, we made slow progress. The multicolor glare of police lights had passed us several times on neighboring streets, but so far we had avoided any direct confrontations. We were now at least three or four miles from the inn and the car we were driving was not one that either Deputy Doug or Mrs. Grimes would be able to describe to the police. But I was still nervous. Whether those flashing lights belonged to state, county, or federal authorities, I was betting that I was right at the top of their Most Wanted list.

I stared over at Jimmy as he hunched over the wheel and struggled to keep the vehicle out of the ditches along the road. "Now, what *are* you doing here?"

He risked a quick glance my way. "I came to see you."

"I sort of figured that out," I replied. "But why? I thought you decided I was barely out of diapers. Did you come to give me a lollipop?"

Even in the dim light I could see the pained expression on Jimmy's face. "Maybe I overreacted. I mean, once you were gone I sort of . . . you know, missed you. A little."

"A little?"

"Yeah, just a little." He glanced around at me again. "So, I sort of decided to see if I could salvage something of the weekend."

"So you flew up to find me?"

Jimmy shrugged. "Not exactly. I missed our flight, and every other plane between St. Louis and Boston was booked, so I sort of drove. Then when I got here, I spent most of the day going from place to place trying to find you."

"So that mysterious man looking for me was—"

''Me.''

I shook my head slowly. ''You drove all the way from Missouri to Vermont just so we could have half a day together?''

''Yeah, I guess I did.'' Jimmy gave a soft laugh. ''And now that I'm here, I do have a couple of questions.''

''Like what?''

He looked up into the rearview mirror. ''First off, when are you going to introduce me to your friend?''

I glanced over my shoulder. In the dimness of the back seat, the vampire looked like a pale patch among the shadows. I suppose I didn't look too different myself. ''She's a . . .'' I started. ''She's . . .''

''Corrine Bancroft,'' the woman suddenly said from the back seat. She leaned forward and offered a white hand over the back of Jimmy's chair.

Jimmy risked taking a hand from the wheel long enough to give her fingers a quick shake. ''Nice to meet you, Corrine.''

I stared at the woman. ''Yeah,'' I said softly. ''Nice.'' I couldn't quite remember the name that Frazier had used for her, but I was very sure it wasn't Bancroft. I had always found it awkward to be saddled with both my real name and a pen name, but on this trip everyone seemed to go by at least two names. ''Corrine has been helping me.''

Jimmy put both hands back on the wheel. ''I see,'' he said. ''Okay, can I ask another question now?''

''Sure.''

''Why are both of you painted up like mimes?''

I wrinkled my nose and tried to think of a tactful way to answer the question. ''It's not paint.''

"Then what is it?"

"It's kind of a disease."

It was a very good thing that we were only going twenty miles an hour. Jimmy slammed the brakes so hard I could hear his foot stomp the floorboards. The car slewed around on the road and traveled at least fifty feet sideways before banking off a heap of frozen slush pushed up by a snowplow, pivoting around ass-backwards, and coming to a rest in the center of the road. I dug my hands into the dashboard and tried to hold on until the car squeaked to a stop.

"What do you mean, a disease?" asked Jimmy. He leaned toward me, his blue-gray eyes peering through the darkness. "What kind of disease makes you look like you've been rolled in flour? Are you all right?"

I gave him credit for asking about me instead of worrying if the disease was contagious. "I'm fine. This is some kind of designer bug. You know, like a germ-warfare thing."

Evidently, Jimmy didn't find this information particularly encouraging. "What do you mean, germ warfare?" he shouted loud enough to rattle the car windows. When I didn't have an immediate answer, he turned to the vampire in the backseat. "Do you know what's going on here?"

"Yes," Corrine replied immediately. "It's called Achromitizing Virus. It's hand-designed to mark the infected so that they're highly visible." Her tone was as dry and clinical as a doctor discussing a bunion.

Jimmy relaxed visibly. "So all it does is make you white?"

"Oh, no," said Corrine. "It's invariably fatal."

"Fatal!" It was my turn to scream. "What do you

mean, fatal?'' My heart did a little dance in my chest and my throat went instantly dry. ''I thought this thing was just supposed to mark you. Like the dye in a bank robbery, remember?''

The vampire leaned back in her seat, disappearing into the shadows. ''As far as I know, that was exactly the intent of AV. However, the engineering of viruses is not quite perfected.'' She paused for a moment. When she started again I was surprised to hear a catch in her voice. ''There were six of us infected. An accident, they said, but a great chance to study the real effects of their new creation.''

She paused again, and this time I could hear her breath coming in deep jerks that were almost sobs. ''What happened?''

''Secondary—'' Corrine stopped and swallowed audibly. ''Secondary symptoms. For some of us it took only hours, others days. My partner, Michael, took weeks to display symptoms. I've been lucky enough to remain at the first stage of the disease—so far.''

Jimmy twisted around in his seat to stare back at her. ''What kind of symptoms are we talking about?'' he asked.

I spoke up. ''I think I can answer that one. Coughing.''

''Yes,'' said Corrine. ''Respiratory distress followed by an acute sun sensitivity, then tiredness, mental degeneration, and eventually death.''

A tingling began to build in my hands and feet and I found it getting harder to breathe. The air of Jimmy's car seemed close, thick, and stale. But this wasn't a new symptom of the disease; this was good old-fashioned panic. "How long?" I asked. "How long once the new symptoms start?"

Cold blue eyes glittered in the darkness of the backseat. "The onset of secondary symptoms seems to represent the midpoint of AV's course. Time from infection to onset appears roughly to equal time from onset to death."

My head began to swim and the numb feeling spread up my arms to my face. There was a pulsing roar in my ears. "Hours," I croaked. "It only took me hours to start coughing."

"I'm sorry," said Corrine.

For a moment there was a unbearable silence in the car, a silence broken only by the pounding of my heart and the roaring of blood in my ears. Hours. Michael Willmeyer had passed on his infection late Friday night. By mid-morning on Saturday, I was already coughing. Were those coughs from the flu I had been carrying around, or was I nearing the end of a very short schedule? I certainly felt exhausted. Was it from little sleep and lots of running around, or was I already on to symptom number two?

Just thinking about the coughing made my throat start to tickle. A moment later, I was doubled over, sputtering through my fingers and struggling to regain control.

Jimmy reached across and put a hand on my back. "What do we do?" he asked. "How do we stop this before Savvy . . . gets hurt?"

The clouds momentarily parted, allowing streams of blue-white light into the car. Corrine's thin face seemed phosphorescent in the sudden glow. "I believe there is a cure," she said.

I wheezed out the last of my coughing fit. "How do we get our hands on this cure?"

"I'm sorry," she said. "I don't know."

I bit my lip and tried to push back my panic long enough to think. "Back at the inn, Frazier said he knew about a cure."

Corrine nodded. "Yes, but he would never tell us."

"Who's Frazier?" asked Jimmy.

"Long story," I replied, then I turned back to Corrine. "What about Coun . . . Willmeyer. Did he know where to find a cure?"

The vampire looked out across the moonlit snowscape around us. "He said he did. Michael and I escaped from the facility in Orange where they were holding what was left of the group infected by AV, but we were separated."

"Orange," I repeated. There was something in that name that tripped a circuit in my brain. "Orange, Germany?"

Corrine shook her head. "No. Orange, New Hampshire. Anyway, Michael had a lot more information than I did. He was going to try and contact others who could help us expose the people that made AV. See that all their facilities were exposed." She shrugged her slim shoulders. "I guess he failed."

"Why Williams Crossing?" I asked. "Was one of the facilities you talked about located there?"

"No," said the vampire. "The Stone River Inn in Williams Crossing was a place Michael and I used to visit often back before we were infected. I've been staying nearby, hoping that Michael might meet me here. But by the time I found out he had come back, it was too late."

I remembered the couple that had appeared over and over on Mrs. Grimes's registry. If that had been Willmeyer and Corrine, then they had been frequent guests, and probably favorites of the innkeeper. Then I remembered the man who had been so scarred and discolored that Mrs. Grimes hadn't even wanted to let him into her inn. By the time I met him, Willmeyer was deep into the final stages of the infection. Even if he hadn't been murdered, Count Yorga had already been living on borrowed time.

Jimmy leaned over and whispered to me. "I take it her friend Michael was your vampire?"

I nodded. "Exactly. He was at the inn when I arrived, but he was killed only a few minutes later."

"What about—" Jimmy started, then he stopped suddenly and looked back. "Hang on a second, looks like company is coming."

I followed his gaze through the back window of the car and saw the pinpricks of distant headlights back down the road. Whoever was coming, they were moving slowly on the icy street, but they were definitely coming our way. "Looks like we need to get moving."

"Right." Jimmy put his hands back on the wheel and cranked the engine. Slowly, he backed the car to one side of the road, flipped it into reverse, then cranked it hard right as he eased forward. It took three such maneuvers to get the car oriented in the right direction again, and by that time the approaching vehicle had halved the distance. Jimmy snapped the car into forward a final time and started off down the road.

I looked back at Corrine. "Who were these people that Willmeyer was trying to contact?"

"I don't really know," she said. "Someone that Michael used to work with, I think. Our escape was really just a stroke of luck. We didn't really have time to plan anything before we were separated.''

''How about this place over in New Hampshire?'' Jimmy suggested. ''The one in Orange? If we went there, would they have the cure?''

Corrine shook her head. ''I don't think so. They were holding us there, but they had no intention of curing us.'' Her white face went hard. ''They just wanted to see how we died.''

''So we're looking for another place,'' said Jimmy. He looked over at me, his lips pressed in a tight line. ''And we may only have hours to find it if we're going to save Savvy.''

''Yes,'' agreed Corrine. ''I'm sorry, but that's pretty much everything I know.''

I knew that wasn't quite true. Corrine—if her name really was Corrine—had to know more about this secret group that had engineered AV. It was clear enough she had met Frazier before, and knew where the fat man's loyalties lay. I suspected that my new vampire pal was still hiding a lot. But when it came to finding a cure for this disease, I guessed she was being as truthful as she could be.

''This place in Orange,'' I said carefully, ''what else can you tell me about it?''

''It was small,'' said Corrine. ''Almost all the facilities are disguised as offices or factories.''

''Was it on the north side of town?'' I asked.

''Not really,'' said Corrine. ''But it was on North Street.''

I felt a new tingle. This time it was excitement instead of fear. ''1428 North Street?''

She thought for a moment, then nodded. "Yes, I think that was it."

I turned to Jimmy. "Do you have a map?"

He nodded. "Check the glove box."

There was a small atlas in the glove box, and a flashlight. I flipped quickly through the pages and tried to focus the light. The type on the pages was tiny, and the flashlight shook in my hand, but it didn't take me long to find what I was looking for. "It's there," I said.

"What's there?" asked Jimmy.

I ran my finger along a line of twisting highway on the map. "Turn the lights on and hit the gas. I think I know where we're going."

FIFTEEN

DAWN CAME WHILE WE WERE STILL DRIVING. ALL NIGHT long, I had drifted near sleep, but each time dreams tried to pull me down, fear jerked me right back up again. Every time I coughed, I tried to gauge it against my previous coughs to calculate the progress of my symptoms. Every random, half-asleep thought might represent the onset of insidious mental decay. Even the exhaustion I felt might be as much a symptom of the disease as from having only a few hours of sleep over the course of three days.

As the sky began to lighten, I looked out the window and wondered if the first rays of sunshine would fry me like *nosferatu*—leaving nothing but smoke and a pile of ash in Jimmy's car. Fortunately, the dawn turned out to be as gray and heavy with clouds as the previous evening—a vampire-friendly sort of day.

In the back of car, Corrine Bancroft was equally awake, her colorless cheek pressed against the window glass and her blue eyes fixed on the countryside slowly rolling past. Jimmy sat grimly behind the wheel, switching from one winding country road to another, slowly working his way toward the destination I had pointed out.

We could have been there in half the time, but I had insisted that we stay off the interstates and main highways. If I had known what the secondary roads in Vermont were like, I would never have set that rule. We spent three hours twisting our way up a range of four-thousand-foot mountains, then just as long curving down toward a broad basin filled with a thickening forest. It was a countryside populated by scattered farms, tiny hamlets, red barns, and covered bridges. Even in the faint moonlight, it was still scenic. From the last turn on the downhill pass, I could see the broad waters of Lake Champlain reflecting the predawn light before we dropped lower and the trees blocked out our view.

"I hope you're right," Corrine said suddenly, breaking hours of silence.

"I have to be," I said. "It's the only thing that fits." I held up the tiny atlas. "In one interview, Willmeyer told me that he had met Newton and Kennedy." I stabbed my finger down on Massachusetts. "And that's just where the facility that Frazier came from is located, Kennedy Lane in the Boston suburb of Newton." I flipped a page. "Then you say that you and Willmeyer were being held in Orange, New Hampshire. Well, in that last interview, he told me that he had been born in Orange. He even gave me the street number disguised as a year. It's obvious that he was using my articles to plant information he wanted to expose about these facilities."

Jimmy whistled under his breath. "You have to hand

it to him,'' he said. ''Passing along secret information by running it right past a few million people. The man had balls of brass.'' He looked over at me quickly. ''I mean—''

''I know exactly what you mean,'' I said. ''In that last interview he also mentioned Shoreham.'' I gave the map a final tap. ''And here it is.''

''Less than ten miles away now,'' said Jimmy. He yawned, and pried one hand away from the wheel long enough to cover his mouth. ''Are you sure this is where we should be going?''

''It has to be,'' I said. I sincerely hoped I was right. The truth was that there were lots of names and dates scattered through the articles I had run on Count Yorga. Any one of them might hide the location of the facility holding the cure. But I hadn't been able to locate any towns or villages nearby that matched the text. I might be misinterpreting the names, or Willmeyer might have been pointing out facilities that were on the other side of the country. Either way, I had gambled my life on a single word.

We turned a final corner, passed a line of well-tended homes, and reached the sign announcing our entry in Shoreham. ''Okay,'' said Jimmy. ''Where do we go from here?''

''I don't know,'' I replied.

Corrine shifted forward in her seat. ''What do you mean, you don't know?''

I shrugged. ''Willmeyer was killed before he could give me anything more. I was just hoping that when we got here, we'd be able to spot it.''

Corrine pressed her white fingers against her face. ''It will be disguised,'' she said. ''It could be anything from a chemical plant to a mattress factory—if it's even here."

"We'll find it," I said with a certainty I didn't really feel. "Just keep driving."

Fortunately for our quest, Shoreham turned out to be an even smaller town than Williams Crossing. There wasn't much more than a single street lined with houses, a few stores, and a handful of bed-and-breakfast inns. I stared at each of them in turn, hoping for some sign that would strip away the facade and reveal an insidious secret producer of genetically enhanced microbes, but the town looked stubbornly normal. A jogger in a Red Sox sweatshirt waved as we went past. Two old men looked at us incuriously from the porch of a Victorian house. Steam wafted above the roof of a small bakery. A mile further on, and we were completely out of town.

Jimmy slowed the car to a halt beside a rolling field where spotted cows worked to extract tufts of grass from around the legs of a large, faded sign. "What now?" he asked. "Do we go back for another pass?"

"There's no point," Corrine said before I could answer. "Nothing in that town could have held even a small facility. I'm afraid we're in the wrong place."

I slumped in my seat, trying to hold down a mixture of despair and fear.

Jimmy reached over and touched me lightly on the cheek. "Let's get on the interstate and head for the nearest city. If we can get you somewhere with a decent hospital, maybe the doctors can do—"

"They can do nothing," interrupted Corrine. "Without the treatment, AV can't be stopped."

Jimmy looked back at her and shook his head. "You don't know that. You said yourself that the people in

Orange were more interested in seeing how you died than in helping you. Maybe some antibiotics would be all it takes.''

Corrine snorted in disgust. ''AV is viral, not a bacteria. Besides, it's a specially crafted organism, immune even to experimental antiviral drugs. Without an equally engineered solution, there is no hope.''

''How do you know?'' he asked.

''I know.''

''How do you know? It could—''

''I know because I helped make it!'' Corrine shouted. She stared down at her hands and her shoulders fell. ''I made it, and now I'm going to die from it.''

I turned away and pushed my tangled hair back from my face. ''Let's go back and make sure,'' I said.

Corrine gave a bitter laugh. ''I already told you, it's not there.''

''It won't hurt us to look again,'' I said. I swallowed a sour taste in my throat and fought back an urge to cough. ''Besides, I don't think I have time to go anywhere else.''

Jimmy looked stricken, but he turned the car into a drive beside the cows and started to turn around. ''Maybe there's something along a side road,'' he said. ''Something we missed.''

I nodded, but I didn't really believe it. A feeling of defeat was creeping over me, erasing everything—even my fear. There was a bone-weary tiredness spilling into my limbs. I knew it was more than vanilla exhaustion. I was entering phase three of the big Achromatizing Virus Elimination Sweepstakes. Soon enough I could expect the joys of feeling my mind fall apart, and after that . . .

I leaned back in my seat and looked outside. If I was going to die, at least the scenery was good. The clouds overhead were breaking up, and the first patches of blue were visible. It was going to be a beautiful last day. I watched the cows pulling grass, and actually felt fairly calm. Then I looked up at the sign.

Jimmy punched the car into reverse, and was just about to pull out onto the highway when I grabbed his arm. "What is it?" he asked.

I nodded toward the sign. My momentary calmness was blasted away by a rising excitement. "This is it."

Both Jimmy and Corrine leaned forward to look out. "Quarry Farms Dairy?" said Jimmy. He looked up the slope at a distant cluster of barns and storage sheds. "What makes you think there's anything special about this place?"

"Look at the next line on the sign," I said.

Corrine read the words aloud. "Robert Quarry, Owner." She shook her head. "I still don't get it."

"Robert Quarry," I repeated. "Count Yorga—the movie Count Yorga—was played by an actor named Robert Quarry." I pointed up the hill. "The answer was right there in his name."

Jimmy let out a noisy breath. "I sure hope you're right." He shifted the car back into forward and started up the slope toward the farm.

I leaned forward, eagerly watching as we drew closer. From the road, there was nothing to see but a few small buildings, but as we passed a screen of trees, larger and more impressive buildings came into view. It still looked like a dairy farm, but it was a *big* dairy farm.

Corrine seemed to be sharing my excitement as we

drew near the first building. "This could be it," she said. "This really could be it."

We bumped our way up the long drive until we reached a refurbished farm house. The hand-carved wooden sign by the door read OFFICE. Jimmy brought the car to a stop and killed the engine. "Okay," he said. "If this is the place, how do you want to handle it? Assaulting some kind of secret base with three people is not exactly smart."

Corrine pushed open her door and immediately started to get out of the car. "Just let me take care of things," she said over her shoulder. "I know how these people think."

I hurried out of the car after her. Jimmy was only a few steps behind me. It was still very early in the morning, and the air was cold enough to sting my sore throat. My breath curled up in front of me and my feet slipped over frozen gravel as we trudged up to the front door. There was a light on over the door, and when Corrine tugged the handle, it opened right away.

Inside was a small room with cheap wood paneling, large posters of cows, and a strong odor of cheese. The only furniture was an overstuffed filing cabinet and a battered green desk liberally covered with multicolored order forms. A small-boned woman in a plaid flannel shirt was scribbling furiously on a form. "Be with you in a second," she muttered. She wrote another few words while Corrine, Jimmy, and I all crowded through the doorway.

The woman looked up with a smile on her lips. "Now, how can I . . . help . . ." Her words trailed away as she looked back and forth from me to Corrine.

"What happened?" she said in a horrified whisper.

Corrine produced some sort of badge from her coat, flipped it out for a moment, then pocketed it again before I could manage more than a blurred glimpse. "We're from the facility at Newton," she said. "There's been an accidental release, and we've been sent here to pick up additional supplies of the matching antiviral."

The woman shook her head so quickly it was more like a twitch than a gesture. "I don't know what you're talking about."

Corrine slammed a white fist down against the desk. "We don't have time to screw around. People are dying."

"I . . ." The woman licked her lips and reached toward a black phone at the corner of the desk. "I'll need authorization," she said. "You'll have to wait here."

"I don't think we can wait," Corrine replied. She reached into her coat again and produced the revolver. She pointed the gun directly at the woman's head. "Now, you see that we get the antiviral we need, or I'll see that you die before we do. Deal?"

The woman sat frozen with her mouth gaping open and her hand halfway to the phone. "Right," she whispered after a moment. "Follow me." She climbed up from her chair and walked toward the back of the office in stiff, shaky steps.

"I thought you knew how these people think," Jimmy whispered to Corrine.

Corrine nodded. "I do. They think they need three forms and twelve signatures just to breathe. If we're going to walk out of here with the vaccine, we're going to have to get it ourselves."

I walked at the middle of the single-file line as we exited the back of the room. The hallway behind the office brought us back outside. The skinny woman walked quickly across the lot toward a very large barn with a roof of corrugated metal. The outside of the building maintained the illusion of a dairy farm, but the doorway was more like something from James Bond. There was a heavy frame of dark metal, a row of tiny LED lights along the left-hand side, and a keypad on the right with about a hundred keys.

The woman stopped by the door. "The agents and antiagents are kept in here," she said.

"So let's go in and get it," I said.

The woman pointed at the keypad. "I don't know the code."

Corrine directed the gun at her head. "How about now?"

"I just don't know," said the woman. "I've never even been inside."

I looked at the heavy door. The rest of the barn looked like boards that had seen a century or two, but I was willing to bet the whole thing was lined with steel and strong enough to thwart access with anything short of a nuclear weapon. "So how do we get in?"

"You could say 'may I,' " replied a new voice.

From around the side of the building strolled Oswald Frazier and Cooper Armistead. Both of them carried semiauto pistols that sported the long vented tubes of silencers. "I would suggest you drop your weapon, Ms. Roenton," Oswald said with infuriating calm. "AV may be killing you slowly, but I can finish the job in a much briefer time."

Corrine hesitated, the revolver gripped tightly in her hand. "You'll kill me anyway, Oswald."

The fat man and his handsome assistant walked

closer. I could see Cooper staring at me with a species of hate and triumph mingling on his face. His male-model looks were somewhat spoiled by a large bruise that stretched from his jawbone to his eyebrow. That, at least, made me feel a little better.

Jimmy leaned in at my side. "Who are these two?" he whispered.

"The bad guys."

"Thanks, I would never have sorted that out."

Cooper waived his gun my way. "Shut up," he said. "Move apart and raise your hands."

I followed directions. Corrine might be armed, but I didn't even have a bed warmer to defend myself this time. "What are you going to do with us?"

"As soon as Ms. Roenton drops her revolver, we'll all take a delightful journey down to Newton." Oswald sighted the barrel of his weapon toward Corrine. "That is, unless your friend decides to be stupid, in which case I'll simply shoot you all right here."

I studied the fat man's face, then looked back at Corrine. "If they take us in, they're just going to watch us die. Aren't they?"

She nodded. "Probably."

A clarity and calm settled over me. One way or another, we were all dead. "Then you might as well go ahead and—"

Brilliant light flooded down from the sky. I cringed and threw my hands over my face. Inside that cone of light, vague shadows moved. Wind whipped over my face and bits of snow and ice hit my exposed skin with stinging force. Then the light was gone as quickly as it had come.

There was a helicopter beside us. It was large, black,

shiny, and completely without markings. The blades that swung back in forth over the top were completely lacking the noise that helicopters usually made. In fact, I wasn't even sure they were blades.

"What's going on?" Jimmy asked. His voice was surprisingly loud.

I shook my head and moved closer to him. "I think it's my UFO."

The woman from the dairy office let out a sudden yelp and went running as fast as her thin legs would carry her. In a matter of ten seconds, she had cleared the driveway, scrambled over a fence, and disappeared into the woods.

Corrine let the revolver slip from her hands and bounce on the frozen ground. "It's over," she said. I couldn't tell if I heard relief or resignation in her tone.

For several seconds, the two gunmen stood frozen by this sudden apparition. Then Cooper Armistead turned and fired his pistol square at the side at the helicopter. I could clearly hear the loud chuff of his silenced pistol, and the metallic ricochet of bullets bouncing from their target. He finished off one clip of bullets, slammed in another one, and emptied it as quickly as the first. So far as I could tell, he didn't even manage to chip the paint.

Throughout his partner's rapid fire performance, Oswald Frazier merely watched. When Cooper's gun made a final dry click, Frazier looked down at the gun in his hand, looked back at the helicopter, then hurled his weapon away and turned to run.

There was an odd, flat sound in the air—like the snapping of the world's largest rubber band—and Oswald Frazier collapsed in a heap. The sound came again, and

Cooper Armistead flung out his arms and tumbled over backwards.

I turned toward the helicopter and tensed as I waited for the strange weapon to fire again. Instead, a hatch popped open in the side and a single man walked out. He was a man over average height and a little more than average weight. He wore a rumpled gray business shirt and a cream-colored tie spotted with a not-quite-erased stain. From his graying hair and the little jowls developing under his chin, I put his age somewhere around fifty.

"Good morning, Ms. McKinnon," he called cheerfully. He raised a hand and waved at me. The wind from the not-quite-helicopter blades blew his hair around, revealing the start of a large bald patch high on his head.

Numbly, I waved back.

The man walked closer. There was a friendly, pleasant expression on his face. "It's nice to meet you at last," he said. He made quick bows to Jimmy and Corrine. "And you too, Mr. Knowles. Ms. Bancroft."

I stared at him in dumb surprise. "Who are you?"

"I'm a fan," said the man from the helicopter. He reached into his pocket and pulled out a scrap of folded newspaper. "I've been reading your work." He extended the paper in my direction and I recognized one of the articles I had written about Count Yorga. "Very interesting reading."

Corrine stepped forward. "Are you the people Michael was trying to reach?"

The man nodded and his expression became more solemn. "Yes. Agent Willmeyer did a fine job. I only regret we weren't able to save him."

"But who are you?" Jimmy asked. He pointed to the

helicopter. ''I've toured almost every military base and taken a ride with almost every military unit in this country, but I've never seen anything like that.''

The man laughed softly. ''I'm sure you all have plenty of questions,'' he said. ''But first I think I have something you need.'' He reached into his jacket and produced a trio of small, bumpy ovals that looked vaguely like the atomizers on old perfume bottles.

''What's that?'' I asked.

''A cure for what ails you,'' said the man. He gestured toward Corrine. ''Ms. Bancroft, you've been infected the longest. Perhaps you should go first.''

Corrine licked her lips, then stuck out her arm. The man from the helicopter reached forward and pressed the bulb against her bare wrist. There was a momentary hiss, and the bulb deflated.

''There,'' said the man. ''I'm afraid it will take some weeks for your body to regenerate the lost pigment, but the other symptoms should stop almost immediately.'' He turned toward me. ''Ms. McKinnon?''

I looked at the little objects in his hand and slowly extended my arm. ''How is it that you already have the cure?'' I asked. ''I thought only the people that made it could fix it.''

''There's a good story in that,'' the man replied. He pressed the bulb against my arm and I felt a momentary prick, followed by a warmth that rushed up my arm and through my body like a fever.

The man turned toward Jimmy. ''Mr. Knowles, AV is not highly contagious, but you should take a dose as a precaution.''

Jimmy seemed to consider this for a moment, then nodded. ''All right. You've already given it to Savvy, you might as well give it to me.'' He held out his arm and the man pressed the final bulb to Jimmy's wrist.

I felt a little dizzy, and wished that there was someplace to sit down. ''That was you that nearly ran me off the road,'' I said.

The man winced. ''We're sorry about that. We had the articles to direct us to other locations, but to find this place, we had no choice but to follow the author.''

''How long have you been watching me?'' I asked.

''Not long,'' the man replied.

Beside me, Corrine suddenly slumped and fell to her knees in the snow. I started to reach for her, but the movement brought a wave of disorientation so strong it was all I could do to stay on my own feet. My head seemed to weigh at least two hundred pounds as I turned back to the man. ''Who are you?'' I asked.

''You've heard of the Secret Service?'' he said.

I nodded. My knees trembled. Just keeping my eyes open was a tremendous effort.

The man smiled. ''We're not them.''

And that was the last thing I heard.

SIXTEEN

"WHEN WE WOKE UP," I SAID, "WE WERE IN THE PARKing lot of a truck stop just this side of Cincinnati."

Bill Genovese nodded. "Move a little to the left. Okay, hold it right there." There was a bright flash. Then another. "And what about your vampire gal?"

"I don't know," I replied. "Jimmy and I were alone in the car when we woke up. Corrine was already gone." There was another flash. I blinked my tired eyes. "Do we really have to do this?"

"Yes, we have to do this," said Mr. Genovese. "It's too bad about this Corrine girl, though. We could have used her." He pursed his lips and tapped a finger against his bearded chin. "Lean in closer. Look more threatening."

I sighed. "Please, this is terribly embrassing!"

Mr. Genovese rolled his eyes. "Look, your story is basically that you were bitten by a vampire, fought it out with secret agents, and were rescued by the men in black."

When he put it that way, my weekend did sound more or less nutsoid, but I had no choice but to nod. "It's true."

"Can you verify any of it?"

That was another difficult question. "Sheriff Loudermilk did die."

Mr. Genovese nodded. "But both his deputy and the local coroner say the sheriff died of natural causes. The man was seventy-nine, Savvy."

I frowned. "I saw him die. Natural causes don't make holes in your head."

"What about the rest of it?" asked my editor. "Can you verify anything else you saw?"

"No," I admitted. I bristled at the unfairness of it all. "Okay, I can't verify every detail in my story, but nothing else that runs in the *Query* has any verification. Why should my story be any different?"

Mr. Genovese's dark eyebrows lowered. Reminding him of the intrinsic sleaziness of our operation was never a good idea. "I thought you were the one that wanted to be different, Ms. McKinnon. Don't you want to be a hot-shot big-time legitimate reporter?"

I ground my teeth together. "Mrs. Grimes will verify that she saw Count Yorga, and she saw me and Corrine."

"And that's precisely the angle we're going to follow up," said Mr. Genovese. He gestured toward the man sitting in a chair beside me. "Now lean in closer. And Harry, try to look frightened!"

I sighed again. The man beside me—a researcher pulled off the celebrity desk to serve as victim in this little tableau, opened his eyes very wide and grimaced while I leaned close and opened my mouth beside his neck. The camera flash popped twice more.

"Okay," said Mr. Genovese. "That should do it."

I stood up straight and rubbed my eyes. "This is *so* embarrassing."

Mr. Genovese grinned. "Ms. McKinnon," he said, "I'm going to make you famous." He held up his hands, framing my face like some ersatz movie director. " 'Reporter Becomes Vampire.' Or maybe, 'Interviewer Becomes Vampire.' " He thought about it for a moment, then shrugged. "Either way, we'll double our circulation."

I shuddered, imagining my bleached-out face gracing a million supermarket aisles from coast to coast. "Can I get cured next week?"

Mr. Genovese looked at me in surprise. "Are you kidding? The *Global Query* is going to be the only paper in the country with a vampire on staff."